MW01282948

All These Subtle Deceits

A Black Wells Novel

C.S. Humble

Ghoulish Books
an imprint of Perpetual Motion Machine Publishing
Cibolo, Texas

All These Subtle Deceits

Copyright © 2022 C.S. Humble

All Rights Reserved

ISBN: 978-1-943720-71-2

The story included in this publication is a work of fiction.
Names, characters, places and incidents are products of the
author's imagination or are used fictitiously. Any resemblance
to actual events or locales or persons living or dead is entirely
coincidental.

Without limiting the rights under copyright reserved above, no
part of this publication may be reproduced, stored in or
introduced into a retrieval system, or transmitted, in any form,
or by any means (electronic, mechanical, photocopying,
recording, or otherwise), without the prior written permission
of both the copyright owner and the above publisher of this book.

www.GhoulishBooks.com
www.PerpetualPublishing.com

Cover by Matthew Revert

For my family, who has given so much

The Astolat Mountain range is in northwestern Colorado. Its peaks are tall and dark, running south to collide with the Rockies and north where they quickly run out, flattening into the plains of Wyoming. Their snow-capped spindles stretch far beyond the gray cloud rack. The snow caps melt in late May. The cold waters come down the crag, engorging the Cam River into a swollen, purple ribbon sewn into the stone.

The Cam hurries during the short, warm months, swinging east and west, down into the Starlight Valley. The river is clear and clean and perilous, white-fanged. The purpling river charges down the slopes, shearing a crescent around the mountain-shadowed city of Black Wells.

You have never heard of Black Wells. It hides in the Starlight Valley, a home to hidden things. A dark metropolis hiding from the rest of the country and the world. A hiddenness meticulously designed. A million and more people live there, most homegrown, but not a few of them transplants.

Those who are born and raised in the city are swift to stay though many of them do not know why. The city compels them to remain. Not because of its grandeur or the promised fortune found in the mineral-rich earth, but something else. Something deeper. Something enrapturing to its natives and seductive to its immigrants. Black Wells captures you. Its allurements conjure a strong chain that wraps around the heart like ivy swallows a trellis. It is a quick and beautiful kind of bondage. A subtle kind of deceit.

Chapter One

Lauren

Lauren **Saunders lay** sprawled out on the cold bathroom tile telling herself she had to get up.

I'm hurt.

She blinked, confused. The room was spinning.

She tasted blood. Blood and something else. Something hard and sharp. A jagged little stone. She rolled her tongue over the pebble. Was that her tooth?

It was.

"Someone . . . " A word fumbled out of Lauren's mouth, no louder than a whisper. "Someone help."

Two hours ago she was drinking overpriced fruity cocktails out of tall cylinders with Janet and Sandra. Celebrating.

Celebrating Lauren's first weekend in Black Wells.

Antonio had sauntered over to the girls' table, gliding over the flashing neon dance floor with a handsome, albeit less-attractive, friend. He had come right over to Lauren and asked her if he could buy her a drink, his voice coated in a thick, Cuban accent.

Antonio, who was nothing like her fiancé Ryan—no, *ex*-fiancé. She had to stop doing that to herself.

Ryan, with his blond hair and shining green eyes who did nothing but *raid* with his pals on whatever fun-come-

3

lately computer game that had just been released. A game that Lauren paid for with money earned from double-shift after double-shift at the hospital. An emergency room nurse's cash spent so Ryan could sit his fat ass in that deluxe gaming chair she'd paid for. Ryan, who made promises of getting a job. Ryan, who told her she was beautiful no matter what the number on the scale said. Ryan, who loved to talk just for the sake of hearing that pinched, whiney voice of his.

Antonio was slender and darkly handsome. Antonio, who had floated out of the writhing crowd of dancers like a prince among subjects. Buying *her* drinks. And it was after drink after drink that Antonio inched closer and closer to her on the rounded leather booth, smelling sweetly of a cologne she had never smelled.

Ryan didn't wear cologne.

Ryan wore aerosol body spray with names like *Hunter's Path* and *Onyx Armor*, stinking like a fraternity schmuck.

Fucking Ryan. Three years wasted on him.

It took Antonio just over an hour to slide his hand over her bare knee under the table. Goose pimples shot up her thigh. He didn't push the touch too far, just rested it on the fresh shaven flesh. She allowed it. Even let him squeeze it as if they had been a romantic item for weeks. There was strength in his hand. A strength Lauren hadn't known in years. Or, come to think of it, ever. She casually slipped her hand away from her glass, letting it drift under the table to fall upon his. They laced their fingers together, each of them looking at the others at the table, laughing and talking and just . . . just touching for the sake of the feeling. A feeling Lauren deserved to feel. A feeling outside of the reach of a pampered man-child—no—a *parasite*.

Synthwave music pulsed feverishly. Lauren's heart thumped along with it.

"Lauren is a nurse. She's coming off a bad engagement.

4

We finally convinced her to move here," Sandra said, grinning ear-to-ear while stirring her straw around in the glass. She was such a freaking loudmouth. A real bitch sometimes with her stupid Jennifer Aniston haircut, wearing so much make-up that when she smiled her foundation cracked like an over-baked cake.

"Oh, that's too bad." Antonio squeezed her knee again, reassuringly.

"Yeah, he was a real jackass who kept telling poor Lauren here that they were going to get married beside a mountain or some dumb shit. What was it again?"

"It was a river," said Lauren, regretting ever telling Sandra anything about anything at any time in her life. "Anyway, Antonio, what do you do?"

Antonio gave his portly friend a smile. "Edmundo and I run a construction company. We build subdivisions all around the county."

"So, you're in *real estate*," said Sandra. "Interesting. You must make lots of money."

Antonio's dark cheeks blushed. He laughed dismissively. "Construction. But yeah, we do okay."

"He's rich," said Edmundo, a consummate wingman.

Everyone at the table laughed and dove deeper into their drinks, telling surface-level stories about who they were. An hour or so later, Antonio let the others spill into a side conversation before he leaned over and whispered a secret into Lauren's ear.

"I like your dress." The heat from his mouth sent a shiver down Lauren's spine. She concealed its effect with a bashful grin.

"Thank you," she replied. "I picked it up this week as a kind of gift to myself. For making the move by myself."

"I would say that I'm sorry to hear about your break-up, but I wouldn't want to start our friendship with a lie."

"He was an asshole. I'm here and that's all that matters to me right now."

"Lucky me," said Antonio, flashing that perfect smile at her again.

It wasn't just the words Antonio said that were charming. It was the way he said them. Relaxed. Cool and confident.

"Dance with me," he said.

Lauren patted him high on the thigh. "Lead the way."

Antonio scooted out of the booth. Lauren followed, doing her best not to notice how close her belly came to grazing the edge of the table. Three complacent years with Ryan and working overtime at the emergency room had led to the poor diet of the overworked. She was fifteen pounds heavier than she should be. But there would be time to take care of that. Maybe if Antonio was the real deal they could work out together, take long jogs or hikes through the Astolat trails. She'd always wanted a guy who was active, not just a slug who sucked on the mothering nipple of low-calorie entertainment.

"Oh, okay," said Janet, pretending to be upset while watching them move toward the dance floor. "We'll just wait here then!"

Lauren playfully turned back to Janet and flipped her off. She took Antonio by the hand and before she knew it they were swimming together in a sea of music and light. She placed her palms on his shoulders and pulled him close. His fingers fluttered over the sequins of her shimmering dress, running the length of her ribs, down the curve of her hip. She waited for him to look into the crowd before she wiped the beads of sweat from her forehead.

Antonio danced with a manly grace, sliding his knee between her legs, letting their thighs grind against one another with the bumping rhythm of the music. Lauren had always wanted something like this. Someone like this. Not someone who wore *Hunter's Path*, but someone who actually hunted the path. Came after her. Lauren chuckled. Comparing Ryan to Antonio was like comparing a warm breeze to a summer heatwave.

"What's funny?" Antonio asked her.

"I was just—nothing."

Antonio rolled his hips into her, allowing his thickness to press into her hip.

Yeah, there was no comparison.

"¿Te puedo besar?"

She hung her arms around his neck. "Is that Spanish?"

"Si."

Lauren laughed.

Antonio laughed too. "It means, 'Can I kiss you?'"

Lauren's smile widened.

She kissed him first, gently. Sweetly.

"Want to do something dangerous?" he asked, then leaned closer. He kissed her earlobe.

Lauren's eyes widened, looking back over to the table where Janet and Sandra were laughing at one of Edmundo's jokes. "How dangerous?"

"Well, it would involve you and me going into one of the bathrooms . . . just the two of us."

Normally the idea of going into a bathroom to do anything other than use it for what it was intended would have repulsed her. But not this time. Something about the two of them alone in a small, public space plunged the heat of her stomach down into swollen anticipation. She had never done anything like that before. The past few weeks had been filled with things she never would have even considered while she was engaged. Moving to a new town before she even had a job. Going out night after night with her friends to dance clubs and bars just for the sake of the fun. That's what this was all supposed to be—fun.

Was it reasonable to go into a bathroom with a man she'd just met, after so many drinks?

No.

And that's exactly why she took Antonio by the hand and led him toward the women's restroom. The idea of going into a men's room was beyond reason. She'd seen

7

and smelled the way Ryan treated their shared bathroom, and she reasonably guessed that was the way all men were. Women's restrooms by comparison were as clean as a grandmother's china cabinet. Lauren pushed them through the crowd eagerly, unapologetically shoving aside everyone in her way. When they reached the door of the one-seater bathroom, Lauren knocked, looking around to check if anyone was watching. No one responded. The coast was clear. Lauren opened the door and pulled Antonio inside. She locked the door behind them and turned.

Antonio kissed her hard and deep, running his fingers up her neck into her hair. His hands cupped the back of her head, lightly clawing at the skin beneath. His other hand squeezed her ribs, pulling the fabric of her dress above her knee. The man's tongue, sweet from liquor, glided past her lips and into her mouth. Not too strong and not too deep. Lauren clamped her nails into the hard muscle of his shoulders. She'd never been kissed like this before. Time passed, their lips greedy, hot, and wet.

Antonio sank his fingers into the dense curve of her hip, mashing her pelvis against him.

A little, hushed moan escaped her lips. A sound she hadn't heard in . . .

Stop thinking about that dipshit.

Antonio pulled back, resting his hand on the damp skin of her neck. He was panting through parted lips that gave him a sensual, predatory appearance. A man that had been offered a great deal and yet still wanted more. More of her.

"Ready for the danger?" he asked.

"Uhm, I thought this was the danger."

He winked. "Part of it."

Antonio reached into the inner pocket of his leather jacket and produced a small, clear baggie filled with what looked like flour.

"What is that?" she asked, a scalpel of worry cutting

8

through her arousal. She felt stupid the moment the question left her mouth. She knew what it was. She'd spent enough time around trembling overdose patients in the ER to know exactly what it was.

"I, uh—"

"You don't partake," Antonio said, the gold flecks in his brown eyes flashing.

"I don't. Look, this is getting a little too crazy for me," she said, inching away from him.

What a fucking waste. Cute, rich guy who thinks I'm hot—of course there's something wrong with him.

"I'm going back to my friends," Lauren said, stepping toward the door.

"Hermosa," Antonio said, sliding those wide shoulders between her and the door. He put his hands around her waist again. "Don't be scared. Do you think I'd let anything bad happen to you?"

Lauren coiled her fingers around Antonio's wrists and gently pushed them away. "Listen, Antonio, I'm going to walk out of this bathroom and pretend like I didn't see the baggie. It was fun, but I'm not okay with this."

"Shh, Hermosa." He reached for her waist again.

"Don't fucking shush me," said Lauren, hardening her glare. "You're going to walk out that door, go over to your buddy and leave me and my friends alone. I'm going to stay here. No harm, no foul."

With those words, all of the things that had been dark and alluring about Antonio turned sinister. His eyes narrowed. The alluring smile melted into a thin, hard line.

She squeezed her hands into fists, ready to knock his balls off if he tired anything else.

But then, to Lauren's relief, the brooding anger melted into disappointment.

"You're right," he said. "I don't suppose we can go back to before my offer?"

"Sorry, Antonio. It's a bust . . . for both of us."

9

"For what it's worth, you are very pretty."

Lauren couldn't roll her eyes hard enough. "Yeah, okay. Good luck with life, or whatever."

Antonio tilted his head, flashing his smile that no longer appeared charming or handsome, just pathetic. Just as pathetic as Ryan.

And in that way, Ryan and Antonio were equals. Two sides to the same bullshit coin.

"Maybe just one kiss goodbye?"

Lauren gave him a 'you've got to be fucking kidding me' look.

"No."

Antonio nodded in defeat, unlocked the bathroom, and exited.

Lauren locked the door behind him. She put her back to the door and sighed. "So fucking stupid." Tears welled in her eyes. *So goddamn fucking stupid.*

"Yeah, go into a public bathroom, while you're drunk, with a strange guy you just met. That's smart. Real healthy behavior." Feeling the weight of the night's drinks on her bladder, she went to use the toilet. Sitting there, she rested her head in her hands, pushing her palms against her eyes hard to keep from crying. The alcohol was making her emotional. That and the major fucking waste of time all men seemed to be.

Lauren lifted her head and cleaned herself. She went over to the sink, let the water heat up, and then washed her hands. Washed them long and thoroughly, trying to scrub away with warm water the cold, sinking feeling in her stomach.

Then a strange thing happened—though she could see the steam coming off the water, she could not feel its heat on her skin. It was probably just the adrenaline shooting through her blood, desensitizing the nerve endings in her extremities. Give it twenty minutes and she'd be right as rain, she knew. Turning off the water, she snatched paper towels out of the dispenser. Drying her hands, Lauren still heard the pitter-patter of the faucet dripping. She examined it with her finger.

Nothing. Only a droplet or two wet her thumb.

"Huh," she said.

Still she could hear the leaky, dripping sound.

That was someone else's problem. It was time to get back to her apartment and sleep off the colossal failure of a night. She dried her hand with the damp paper towels again and turned to throw them away, but she caught something in the corner of her eye. Something in the mirror.

There were three shapes behind her.

Each of them faced away from her, lined up along the bathroom wall. Their feminine figures stood naked. Their paler-than-milk, almost blue skin was distended, beaded with water. Each of them had long, dark hair running past their shoulders. Fat droplets fell from twisted, tangled strands, dripping onto the bathroom tile.

"I—" Lauren's breath caught like a hook in her throat.

The three figures moved in unison, their bloated hands rising to cup their unseen faces. They began to sob. A flat, droning moan.

"Are you . . . "

Their hands snapped down to their sides again, the sobbing ceasing immediately. Slowly and in unison, they turned. Turned only their heads toward Lauren. The vertebra of their spines crunched like brittle autumn leaves deep within their cold, swollen skin. Their gazes fell on Lauren, each of them peering with rheumy eyes, swollen-white.

The three naked women whirled on Lauren, their mouths breaking open into wide, prey-like keening. The screams so loud and abrupt that it pushed Lauren back in shock. Her heel squeaked against the tile, sending her off-balance. She fell, reflexively squeezing her eyes shut.

11

Red and white sparks shot through the darkness.

It was there, on the ground, that she felt the smooth, cadaver-cold fingers of rough hands mash her face, invade her mouth. Then, fingers curled to claws, they raked jagged nails between her breasts, snagging the neckline of her dress before descended further, clawing her bare thighs. Lauren screamed and thrashed her legs, kicking wildly. She opened her eyes to see . . .

Nothing.

There was no one there.

The room was spinning, but it slowed and she took a deep, sucking breath.

"Someone . . . someone help."

There was no one.

A lance of pain shot through Lauren's jaw. She gently pressed against her cheek to make sure her mandible and maxilla were intact. Her tongue ran over what was, without question, a chipped tooth jabbing into the soft tissue of her cheek, caught between it and her gum line. She scooped her tongue against her gums, fishing it out. She held it between trembling, pinched fingers, determining it to be the entire top half of a molar. Without knowing why, she let the tooth go. Breathing became heavy and erratic. Her whole body began to shake involuntarily and something was building inside her stomach. Something between nausea and something more, something that became wind in her lungs. Something that made her mouth open painfully wide.

Lauren screamed.

She scrambled off the wet tile, her feet skittering against the floor. Frantically, she fumbled at the lock on the door, finally unlatching it. The door swung open and she ran.

Past the dancers in the flashing, neon light of the booming club.

Past the bar, where patrons shot shocked glances over at the girl who was screaming out of the bathroom.

Past the bouncer, the door, and the velvet rope line. Out into the snowy night, she ran, still screaming. She could not stop screaming.

Chapter Two

William

William Daniels stood in the doorway of St. Patrick's Cathedral, accompanied by a short, hawkish man almost half his age. There in silence, in the arch of the alley exit, they waited. Thunder rumbled. Droplets thick and heavy pounded an overflowing dumpster and slick, black garbage bags. There was a ripe stench of sewage that even the persistent rain couldn't dampen. If anything, it made it worse.

"Seminarian?" William asked.

"Deacon." The young man smiled with confidence.

William lifted his eyebrows. "Ah, ordained. Deacon . . . "

"No need for titles with me. I'm Jason Trask."

"Jason, look. I appreciate the gesture, but you don't need to wait."

"It's no trouble. Really."

"Simon insisted, I'm sure."

The deacon's smile soured. "No need for titles with me, but His *Eminence*," said Trask, "*Cardinal* McMichael requested that I attend to your exit. Regardless, no one should have to wait alone. Certainly not after what you did for the boy . . . " Trask trailed off. After a deep, composing breath he found it again. "In any case, your ride will be here any minute now. And like I said, it's no trouble."

14

The deacon opened his mouth, as if to ask a question, but stopped himself, unsure.

Veins of lightning illuminated the alley pavement where a little gray stream carried garbage and old church leaflets into the rectangular darkness of a storm drain. The sound of the churning waters drowned out by the fresh rumble of angry thunder. Maybe there was something in the strength of the storm that gave the deacon the courage to say what he'd previously fell short of saying. Whatever it was, William didn't know.

What he did know was the question Jason would ask.

All the priests-in-training asked questions, right after they confirmed—

"You're Father William Daniels," Jason said. "Um, the exorcist."

"Not officially."

"You were defrocked?"

"Being excommunicated by the Pope has that effect. It also means that after you do your friend of 20 years a favor, they ask you to use the *back* door." William stabbed his thumb toward the closed, oak-paneled door behind them.

"Yes, well, His Eminence doesn't want people—"

"Don't sweat it. Like I said, being proscribed by His Holiness means they're happy to call you for a solid, but not expect an invitation to the pancake supper fundraiser."

"Can I ask you a question?"

William watched a white, vintage Mustang roll into view, then stop across the street, blinker winking against the rain. "Better hurry, that's my lift."

"What was that sound? While you were in the room. What was that?" There was fear there. Fear and uncertainty.

William looked at the deacon, searching the young man's eager look. A yearning to confirm what his suspicion detected. "You're an ordained deacon of the Church, Jason. You've read your Bible. You know why the family brought their son to the Cardinal. And you know who I am." He cocked his head. "Put all that together and you have some theories as to what makes a sound like that."

The color in Jason's face drained almost paper-white. "Wait. You're saying it was an actual—"

"What I'm saying, Jason, is that you're young and religiously educated. Brave enough to ask the question. But, you're asking the wrong question. And asking the wrong person."

Jason furrowed his otherwise lineless brow in confusion.

William continued. "The question you should be asking yourself is, would you want to be in a room with something that makes that sound?" He hardened his eyes on the young man. "Take your time on it. Then, stew on it a little bit more. Because being in that room is much, much worse than it sounds."

William pulled back a bit when he saw Jason's eyes shift left, right, then left again as his breathing accelerated. William lifted his palm toward the deacon, a calming gesture. "When you think you've got a good answer, you take it to *His Eminence*. And if after that, you're still an ordained deacon on his way to playing major-league priest for the Catholic Church in this diocese, you should check yourself into a fucking psychiatric ward."

Jason's mouth fell open.

"You've still got a choice on what kind of life you're going to live," said William.

"I've chosen to serve God, *Mister* Daniels. There is no more valorously rewarded life."

William tilted forward at the waist, leaning the weight of his countenance hard on the young deacon. "It's not like the movies *in* the room, kid. Not even like it is in the book of Acts. If it were, you'd have been in the room. Not me."

After having waited for a slew of cars to pass, the white Mustang turned into the alleyway. The car's chrome trim, beaded with rain, glimmered as if encrusted with diamonds. Fog on the windshield obscured a red-headed woman's face behind the wheel.

William flipped up the collar of his long, gray coat. He slipped his matching, black-banded hat onto his head. Then, he popped the deacon on the shoulder. "Here's a free piece of advice, Jason. Go serve God someplace where he still gives a shit."

William stepped out from under the archway into the pelting rain, leaving Jason behind.

Jason called out, "I am not afraid. God will protect me."

William didn't look back. "If you say so." He opened the car door and slid into the passenger seat.

The woman in the car waited for him to put on his seatbelt before she spoke. "Alley, huh? Really gave you the papal treatment."

"Thanks for the lift, Sherry," said William as he removed his rain-soaked hat.

Sherrilyn Foote was in her mid-fifties, but you couldn't see it in the brightness of her green eyes, the smoothness of her skin. The three-hundred-dollar hair dye job didn't hurt, either.

"I'm not a taxi service, you know. When are you going to get a new car?"

"I've got a car. It's in the shop."

"Yeah, I know you've got a piece of shit that you loosely categorize as 'a car'. You need a new one. Could even get it in black, match that uniform of yours."

"It's not a uniform. They're priestly vestments."

"Aren't those vestments supposed to come with a clerical? Oh, wait, that's right, the Pope fired you."

"The Pope doesn't fire people. He excommunicates them."

"Sounds like a fancy word for fire."

"You love fancy words."

"Yeah, but I never use a fifty-cent piece when a nickel will do. Who was the priest? He's cute."

"Ordained deacon. Priest in training. Can we go, please? Get out of this god-forsaken weather."

Sherry smiled a smile that had cost her at least ten grand. "This is Black Wells, Will. It isn't god-forsaken weather. It's just *the* weather. Home?"

"Can we stop by my office first? Have some things I need."

Sherry put the car in reverse. Reaching over, she laid her arm over William's shoulder, instead of the passenger seat, then turned to look out the back window. Slowly, she pulled out of the alleyway with the rain slapping the convertible's roof. "Don't mind my saying, but you look terrible. Bad one in there?"

"They're all bad, Sherry."

"Kid?"

"Eleven-year-old boy." William rubbed his eyes.

"Christ. You win?"

"Loosely categorized, sure. If he has good parents and a shrink he'll probably recover."

Sherry pulled the Mustang into the street. She clawed her nails along William's shoulder playfully. "What do you say you and me get out of the city? Take a flight to San Francisco, get a hotel room. Friends with benefits for a week."

"Sherry."

"I'm just saying, you look like a man who could use a little spoiling. And I'm really, really good company," she said, running her fingernails soothingly through his hair.

"Sherry."

"Fine. Fine," she said, slipping her hand off his shoulder. "We'll call it a maybe."

William sighed. "I appreciate the gesture and the lift. I just have a lot on my plate right now and it's already the end of the month."

Sherry clicked her tongue. "Maybe you won't get a letter this time."

"Teresa's letters are the only consistent thing in my life right now—"

"Umm, excuse you?"

That got a chuckle out of him. "And you and Karl, of course."

"Thank you."

"But, it's the end of the month. There's going to be a long, brown envelope in my box with her handwriting all over it."

"I'm free tonight," she said. "Let's have dinner at least."

William turned and looked at her. The starkness of her wide smile made him grin. "You're persistent."

"And a knockout," she said, winking at him.

"Yep."

"And rich."

"Loosely categorized."

Sherry laughed louder this time, the sound was bright and wild. "Why William Daniels, was that an insult?"

"Mostly a joke," he said, and gently patted the back of her hand resting on the shifter.

"I'm rich as hell," she said. "I could buy your apartment complex, and your little rented office space ten times over if I wanted to."

"Hold on," William said, looking out the windshield, all the levity sucked out of his voice.

"What is it?"

"See that lady there?"

"Where?"

"She's standing on the steps to my office building."

"I see her, but why am I holding on?"

"She's standing in the rain."

"So?"

"So, it's raining and she's got an unopened umbrella in her hand."

"You're paranoid," said Sherry, parking the car along the curb of William's office building.

"No," he said, looking back at her. "I just know a customer when I see one. Tell you what, drop me here. Even if she isn't waiting to see me, you can pick me up here for dinner. Lots of work to do."

"Give me a ring when you're ready, okay?"

"Will do. And, Sherry . . . "

"Yeah?"

"Thanks for everything."

Sherry fluttered her lashes at him, overplaying her gratefulness. She kissed her fingertip and pressed it against his cheek. "Good luck, Will."

"Jury's still out."

William got out of the Mustang and walked over to the woman standing in the rain.

She was young, no more than twenty-five by his estimation, with cream-colored skin, rounded cheeks, and eyes as blue as they come. Eyes shadowed with heavy bags underneath that shone even brighter against the darkness of her wet, auburn hair. When she looked at him, the gaze focused on him, yet somehow remained distant.

William knew the look all too well. The look of a person lost in the fatigue of despair.

"Excuse me, ma'am," William said as Sherry's car pulled back out into the street. "Do you need some help?"

"I tried buzzing into the building, but didn't get an answer. I'm looking for William Daniels," she said, shivering against the wet cold.

"I'm William. Sorry about the door. No walk-ins allowed. Building rules. Please—"

"My name is Lauren. I got your information from Doctor Irvin."

William's jaw clenched.

Mira Irvin was a psychiatrist. More importantly, she was *his* psychiatrist.

20

"I see," he said.

"Please," she said, her lip starting to tremble. "Something happened to me. Doctor Irvin said you might be able to help. Please don't think I'm crazy."

"Having a conversation in this rain would be crazy, Lauren. Why don't we go inside to talk?"

"I didn't mean to show up without an appointment, I just—"

"I've got all sorts of time. Come on," he said, and escorted the young woman up the steps and into his life.

Chapter Three

Lauren

"What kind of consultant?" Lauren had asked Doctor Mira Irvin during their eleventh appointment since the incident in the nightclub bathroom.

"A ... specialist," Mira said, dismissively, while straightening in her chair. She was a slender, professional woman with skin desperate for a tan and pecan brown hair starting to silver at the roots. "Lauren, under normal circumstances I would never do what I am about to do, but after last week's ... situation, I think an outside consultant is necessary."

"Is he a colleague?"

"We have a ... professional relationship. You and I have been meeting for almost six months and typically I would prescribe you with a low-grade antipsychotic to help with what I initially diagnosed as hallucinations." Doctor Irvin crossed her legs and looked down onto the legal pad in her lap. "But, like I said, our last session was anything but typical."

"Right ... "

"You don't have to be embarrassed, Lauren. Or afraid. Fear and shame aren't tools of recovery. They're metaphorical demons that, through hard work, we deserve to have exorcised from our patterns of thinking."

"Yeah? Well, what about the non-metaphorical things haunting me?"

Mira smiled apologetically. "Not my department, I'm afraid. I've had patients tell me they could hear the devil whispering to them. A young man once told me that he could take me to the place where he was abducted by a UFO. And on more than one occasion I've had patients suddenly start to scream, screaming as if my life were in mortal peril from some kind of apparition or evil spirit standing behind me. A spirit only they could see. This is Black Wells, so superstitions like that run pretty deep. But . . . " Mira paused, reaching with her left hand to comfort a palsied tremor taking over the right.

"Sorry," Mira said. "It comes and goes."

"Please, don't apologize. It isn't because of my—"

"No, it's an old condition. But, what I was going to say is, I've heard all of these things from patients—whispers, abductions, hauntings. But I've never *seen* anything from a patient that I could not explain with psychological medicine." She paused, taking a deep breath. "Until last week."

Lauren's gaze fell to the floor, where she saw a scarlet and gray rug. A new rug. The previous rug had been gold and crimson and obviously very expensive. And it had been ruined in the "attack", when Lauren had lost control of her bladder.

She had lost control of everything while suspended upside-down four feet in the air.

"The rug was a gift from my now ex-husband. You practically did me a favor." Mira looked back down at the legal pad. "You said you aren't religious and do not consider yourself a spiritual person. You were raised Baptist by your parents, but you quickly moved away from that faith tradition during college."

"Right . . . it all seemed silly at the time. Guy up in the sky, white beard. Like a more judgmental version of Santa Claus."

"Be ready for Mr. Daniels to broach the subject of your

spiritual beliefs. I am assuming they will be a part of his line of questioning."

"Sure, that's no problem. Will he be here during my next session?"

"Ah, no," Mira said, again with that apologetic smile. "I'm going to provide you with his office address. Your best bet is to try and catch him between his normal business hours. He doesn't like phones." She produced a card from her writing folio.

Lauren took the card and examined the red-brown ink stamped into the bone-white surface. It read:

WILLIAM DANIELS
INTERCESSOR AND CONSULTANT
ECCLESIASTICALLY CENSURED

On the back was an address and office hours. No phone number.

Mira had been spot-on. The moment Lauren and William got out of the rain and under the golden archway into the foyer of the building, the tall, gaunt man turned to her and bluntly asked, "Are you Catholic?"

Lauren's eyes widened with a nervous shake of her head. "Umm, no. Does that matter?"

"Only if you are," he said, peeling himself out of his long, gray coat.

He folded the coat over his arm, revealing to Lauren what reminded her of the kind of clothes she saw priests wear in the old horror movies that Ryan had forced her to sit through. Movies like *The Exorcist* and *Salem's Lot*. There was something missing from the outfit though. The open gap at the throat, which was supposed to have some kind of white collar.

The man's wet, leather shoes squeaked across the black and white checkered squares of the marble floor, where he walked toward a wall of small brass doors. Post office

24

boxes. William reached into his pocket and produced a set of keys that jingled loud and tinny in the empty lobby.

Lauren started to feel nauseous at that sound . . . no, not the sound.

It was about to happen.

She could feel that . . . that indescribable sensation she felt right before—

Suddenly, they were there. The pale blue women were standing right next to William Daniels. Their milky stares examining him. Then, like so many times before, each of them in unison opened their mouths to wail.

Lauren grit her teeth, quickly turning away from the wall. Her breath seized in her throat. Swallowing hard, she began to count back from ten.

When she got down to one, she opened her eyes.

Thankfully, William was the only person looking at her. "Everything all right?"

Lauren sighed. "Yeah," she said, trying to relax. "I think so." She scanned all three stories of the interior wall, where the dimpled tile curved into a great dome. The dome terminated at the center of the ceiling in the form of an immaculate rose window. The window's colors were muted against the rainclouds still thundering outside, but that did not stop her from admiring the bronze-trimmed man etched into the glass. No, not a man.

He had wings.

Pearl-white wings made the man an angel.

"Oh, wow," Lauren said, admiring the glass mosaic. A blue robe and gold spear accentuated the pink glass of the angel's face. He was falling, or so it appeared, descending with his spear thrusting down. Toward what, she did not know. "What's that?"

"It's St. Michael the Archangel." William reached wrist-deep into the open mailbox. He produced a stack of white envelopes, rubber-banded together and a large, brown envelope. "And you not knowing who it is confirms one of my first suspicions about you."

She swallowed, her throat dry. "Which is?"

"You tell the truth." His tight line of a mouth tried to grin, but it just made his frown lines appear more pronounced. "Almost every Catholic has seen that image, or at least one like it. This one in particular is an interpretation of Raphael's *Le Grand Saint Michel*. Interestingly enough, with this version the artist left out a key figure in the piece."

"That being?"

"Lucifer. The enemy whom St. Michael is casting out of paradise. Protestant?"

"No." Lauren shook her head. "I'm Baptist."

William's blonde-brown eyebrows lifted and he blinked at her.

"Well, a lapsed Baptist, I guess. I haven't been to church since I was 15."

"Lapsed Baptist." He sniffed. "That's funny. In an oxymoronic kinda way."

Lauren sensed that he was having a bit of fun at her expense. With all the shit she had endured the last six months, she wasn't going to put up with it. She'd stood in the rain for over an hour waiting for this asshole to show up during his own office hours, and for all she knew he'd just rolled out of bed. "Mr. Daniels, I'm here because something in my life is very, very wrong. And I am very afraid. So do you think we could cut the sarcasm?"

William winced, furrowing with mild embarrassment. "I am sorry. I've had a very long day and it's just after noon. Tell you what, why don't we head up to my office. I'll put on some coffee and you can tell me your situation. Where, I promise," he said, placing his hand over his heart, "I will listen without interruption or religious jack-assery."

The apology felt sincere to Lauren. The truth of that sincerity didn't come from his words or his tone, but from the clearness of his fatigue. The gauntness of his face, which edged toward masculine frailty, mixed with the dark circles under his . . . and that was when she first noticed it. Surely she had seen it when she met him, but it was only now, when he slanted his eyes to look at her after his apology, that she registered with absolute clarity that William Daniels's eyes were two different colors. Set deeply socketed just above the dark, half-moon bags under them, the left was slate blue. A blue that reminded Lauren of the storm clouds raging presently outside. The right eye was so much brighter, a piercing green. Almost the color of mint leaves.

Though he was not particularly a good-looking man, his full gaze was wholly arresting. Almost frightening.

"I'm tired, too, Mr. Daniels and—"

"Call me William. Or, Will is fine."

"A cup of coffee would be nice, William."

"Follow me up," he said, turning toward an ornate, metal staircase lined in blackened steel and polished brass.

Lauren walked just behind him, climbing the stairs, quickly turning away from the wall to focus on the balustrade. The nausea was there again, not overwhelming, but somewhere at the edge of her, somewhere elusive. She let her fingers curve around each smooth, brass baluster lining the stairs. They glowed like molten gold in the yellow light falling from caged Edison lamps. Each step they took snapped with a metallic clatter that punctured the otherwise eerie quiet of the office building.

"Where are all the people?" Lauren asked. "The other businesses?"

"I'm the only resident of this building," he said, turning toward a dark, wooden door. A sheet of frosted glass was set in the wood, brandishing black letters trimmed in gold. Black letters mirroring the same words as his business card.

William opened the office door, leaned past the frame

27

and flicked a switch. With a loud snap, yellow light illuminated a simple waiting room. He stepped aside. "Only me and the mail lady have a key."

The sickening feeling in her stomach swelled. She didn't trust this person, didn't know what he would say if she told him the truth, and certainly didn't like the idea that he was the only one in the building who could lock the building's front door.

Or unlock it.

Had he locked the door when they came inside? Lauren couldn't remember.

"Is everything okay, Ms. Saunders?"

Lauren convinced herself that her anxiety and paranoia were a part of her own inability to sleep well. Lauren did trust Dr. Irvin and, after all, she was the one who had suggested that Lauren see this strange man with the strange eyes inside of what might be his strange, art deco murder-castle of an office building.

Lauren felt her mouth filling with saliva, her stomach bubbling like a pot brought to boil.

"William, I want to tell you that I am very uncomfortable right now. I didn't know we would be the only people here."

William nodded, stretching one side of his mouth downward. "I have this effect on people."

"No, no . . . " Lauren tried to vocally backpedal. "It's not just you, it's just . . . just everything lately has me afraid. Like I'm not in control of my own mind." Lauren's bottom lip, wet with saliva, began to tremble. She clenched her jaws tightly together, so sick and goddamn tired of crying all the time about the same thing over and over again. But despite her best effort to keep the tears from welling in her eyes, they found their way onto her round cheeks, spilling to her chin. "Like I'm losing my life one night at a time to these . . . these *fucking* things that won't leave me alone. These *women*."

William lifted a single, thin finger into the air, a polite gesture. "I want to hear your story, Lauren. Can I ask for two minutes before you tell it to me?"

"It's fine," Lauren said, her voice sounding thick and stuffy with the mucus filling her sinuses. She scowled at herself for feeling like this. She ran the back of her hand along her neck where tears were forming in a fold that at some point over the last few months had developed under her chin. "I feel so stupid for crying all the time."

William reached into his coat pocket. From it he produced a crisp, white handkerchief. He handed it to her. "I'll be right back," he said. "Don't go anywhere."

Lauren placed the linen cloth against her face, wiping away the wet streaks along her cheeks and dabbing at her running mascara. Great. Now she wasn't going to just sound like an insane person, she'd look like one of those raccoon-eyed serial killer women on those early afternoon TV movies.

A few minutes later, after cleaning her face, Lauren caught the distinct aroma of fresh coffee brewing. That soothed her stomach. Then, through the door, a leather club chair on rollers pushed its way onto the marble floor of the hall. William came through the door next, guiding the chair behind where Lauren was standing.

"Sec," he said, then disappearing into the office once more.

He brought out a slender, round-top wooden table and then rolled another chair to face opposite of the one he'd brought out for Lauren. He reached into his suit and produced a leather pouch, which he set on the table before walking back into the office. When he came out for the last time, he was carrying a sterling coffee serving set on a matching platter, adorned with two navy-dyed china saucers and cups trimmed in gold. The gaunt man with surprising grace, and a clear flair for formality, set the platter down next to the pouch.

29

"Please, have a seat," he said.

"But, I'm all wet and—"

"Oh, right!" From out of his back pocket he produced a hand towel. "Sorry, best I've got."

Lauren thanked him and set the towel on the seat. She sat down. The chair was tufted leather, because it had been inside the heated building it was smooth and warm. Lauren sank into it, the smell of the coffee driving away the cold of the rain on her skin and the churning of her guts.

"Lauren, I'm going to begin our professional relationship with a confession," he said, pouring them equal cups of steaming coffee. He sat in the chair opposite her. "I have several vices, one of which is that I am a pipe smoker. But, seeing as I make the rules here in this office building, I need only your permission to indulge in what is a disgusting habit."

Lauren shook her head. "I don't mind."

"Tremendous." He took the pouch off the table into his nimble hands, zipped it open, and plucked a fat, acorn-bowled tobacco pipe into his fingers. He set the pipe on the table and snapped open the other side of the pouch. Nimbly, he pinched black ribbons of maple-sweet-smelling tobacco and gently packed it into the bowl.

William clenched the pipe between his teeth. "You're sure?"

Lauren chuckled. "Sure."

"Thank goodness for little graces," he said, the pipe bouncing with his words. He struck a match on the bottom of his black oxford and lit the tobacco with slow, achingly gentle pulls. The flame caught the tobacco, transferring the fire from match to bowl, wafting a comforting aroma over the already relaxing smell of the coffee.

The man curled his hand around the bowl and pulled long and slow, a deep satisfaction masking his face. Blue-gray smoke flooded out of his nostrils, then out of his mouth in a cascading cloud. With that first, true inhalation accomplished, he turned and looked at Lauren. His mismatched eyes shined sharp in the Edison light. The way he leaned into the corner of the wing-backed chair suggested a great deal of time was spent there.

"Second confession, Lauren." He said her name like they had known one another for years. Familiar. Matter-of-fact. "My name is William Daniels. I am a spiritual intercessor and one of the leading occult-based consultants in the world. I am an exorcist by trade and I have been excommunicated by the Holy Roman Church." He took another long drag from the pipe.

"Excommunicated?"

He sighed, laughing at himself. "Think of it like the Pope fired me."

"The Pope fires people?"

"If they break certain rules, yes. Which I did."

"Like what? Did you kill someone?"

"Surprisingly, that one doesn't always get you fired. But, no, I was charged with something called the desecration of the Eucharist."

"That's the bread and the grape juice. I know that. We did that in the church where I grew up," she said, then sipped at her coffee.

"Grape juice . . . " William shook the rest of the thought away, as if remembering his promise about sarcasm. "To put it plainly, Lauren, I help people who have experienced something unfamiliar to their perceived reality. These things include possession, hauntings, supernatural abductions; things like that. If Doctor Irvin sent you directly to my office, it means you had an encounter that her medical experience cannot explain. What I would like, Lauren, is for you to tell me what happened to you. Tell me when it happened. And if at any point you think you'll sound crazy or silly telling me any particular detail, I want you to remember that my current job title is: exorcist."

Lauren nodded slowly. The warm cup felt comforting

in her hands and her fears about being alone with William shifted into something else entirely. Something not quite close to trust, but close enough to safety. And so, as she had done before with Doctor Irvin three times before, Lauren went into stark detail about the three women who she had seen in the bathroom of that nightclub. The women who Lauren saw standing in room after room, always ready to scream.

She had seen them standing against the wall of mailboxes while William gathered his mail. Seen them standing, naked and silent and brooding, against the wall inside of the lighted waiting room. And again, she saw them now.

Standing behind William Daniels.

Chapter Four

William

William had been waiting all damn night and morning to have that bowl of tobacco. The flavor of rum and maple and oak smoothed every wrinkle of frustration. The nicotine pressed his thoughts together sharp and straight as a dry-cleaned dress shirt. The caffeine compounded the nicotine's effect.

"I want you to remember that I just told you that my current job title is: exorcist," he said. That line always cut through the tension with potential clients. Fear varied from client to client, but every person feels ridiculous trying to convince someone else that the improbable story they are telling is the actual, honest-to-God, truth. Most of the time, William thought.

There were *actual* people who simply had a compromised psychological immune system. Without treatment over a long period of time, hallucinations seem as real as the genuine article. Those were the hardest cases for him. Mostly because they were the cases he could not take. He could not help those people. That incapability wounded him. Hurt him the most when he had to refer those people to Doctor Irvin. It never went well.

Lauren Saunders was the first person Doctor Irvin had referred to *him*. That felt like a breach of doctor/client privilege. He didn't know how he felt about it at the moment, but he knew for damn sure he'd bring it up at their next session. Right now, he needed to focus on Lauren. Actively listen.

It was very clear to William, after he tried to encourage Lauren to tell her story, that she did not have any kind of mental affliction. When he looked up from his steaming cup to give her his full attention, he saw absolute terror on her face. There is a fine line between 'thinking' you see something supernatural and 'experiencing' something supernatural. Much the same as a person camping in their tent *thinks* they might hear a bear versus the person who, walking along, suddenly locks eyes with one while alone in the woods. The two moments share the same elements, but the horror of one greatly exceeds the other.

Lauren had locked eyes with something behind him.

Something, whatever was haunting Lauren, had followed her inside.

The look on her face gave William the sensation of someone sticking a long, cold needle into his ear.

He whipped his head around.

Nothing.

"Lauren," he said quickly, "what are you looking at? Right now, tell me what you see."

Lauren opened her mouth to say something.

No words came out.

Her mouth widened, as if Lauren was going to yawn. Widened further, as if she were going to scream. The blue of her eyes rolled to white. Her head seemed to dislocate from her backbone, as if it were too heavy for her spine, slowly drifting and tilting unnaturally against the chair. She dropped her coffee. The saucer and cup shattered, sending fragments of blue china and black coffee across the floor.

William jumped up from his chair. "Lauren!"

The woman's jaw widened further. A loud pop echoed from some place deep in her skull. She began to moan. Her fingernails dug into the chair, peeling the fine leather back, revealing the downy yellow cushion inside. Her lips drew back so far that William saw the smile her decaying skeleton would brandish a hundred years from now.

He placed his hand on her arm, checking her pulse. "Lauren," he said, calling her name over and over. Her heart was racing, but it hadn't stopped. That was the good news. The bad news was that it was racing so furiously that it might explode.

"Lauren! Come back. If you can hear me, you've got to come back. Listen to my voice!"

The silver platter of coffee exploded off the table. An invisible force sending it flipping into the air. The platter, the carafe, and William's cup all slammed against the wall.

"Goddamn it!" he screamed as hot coffee scalded the back of his hand. When he looked back to Lauren, he saw that her lips were drawn back so fiercely that her chapped lips had split, filling with blood.

"Lauren, listen to me! Do you hear my voice? Listen!" Lauren sucked in a long, ragged breath, like the final inhalation of a dying asthmatic. Her legs kicked at him, her heel coming down hard on his toes.

"Lauren!"

The woman's vacant eyes fluttered, rolling down so that the vein-laced whites were replaced with her sparkling blue irises. And then, as happened upon escaping a diviner's well, Lauren used all the air inside her to scream.

William backed away and let her get all the screaming out of her system.

It took a very long time. But, eventually, Lauren's screaming shuddered from keening to sobs. Sobbing that shook to trembling apologies William refused to accept. Her hands shot along her thighs, checking for what William did not know. The woman was still crying when she managed, "What the hell *is happening to me?!*" Her quaking fingers fluttered over her lips, as if she were trying to cage the possibility of another scream.

William placed a hand gently on her shoulder. "Take a breath."

Lauren obeyed.

"Good, now another. Good. One more."

The woman, now somewhat composed, looked at him, exhausted. Drained.

"Do you have any history of psychological illness in your family, Lauren?"

She wrinkled confusion at him. "Not that I know of."

"A sibling that had a nervous breakdown during puberty? Uncle who thought he was being chased by a clandestine arm of the government? Black helicopters-type stuff. Or anyone ever say that they saw things other people couldn't see?"

"Umm—no."

"And this question will seem odd, but . . . " He took a deep breath. "Lauren, have you been dabbling in any kind of spiritualism or made contact with any kind of entity that might be categorized as 'other-worldly'?"

"What?! *No*."

"Okay. Lauren. I want you to tell me in as stark of detail as possible what you *have* been seeing over the last six months. But before you do, I want you to know something . . . "

Lauren braced herself.

"You are absolutely not going crazy. Whatever these attacks are, they are real. And I can help you with them, but—"

"But, what?"

"I cannot stop them. Not entirely. At least, not yet." William examined the shards of china splayed out on the ground. "But, I do know of someone who can protect you from them."

After Lauren had described the women to William, they left the building. He offered to drive. He angled

Lauren's green, four-door sedan away from his office through the pelting rain.

"Listen," he said as he flicked the wipers to their highest setting, "There are a number of possibilities to explain what is happening to you, and I don't want to speculate on any of them right now because I don't want to worry you until I know exactly what kind of situation we're dealing with. What I can say is that these trances you go into, they are likely only going to get worse with time, unless we get you into a protective barrier that keeps them at bay."

"What, like, a church or something?"

"Not exactly, but I like where your head is at. I have a . . . a friend who has such a place. She and I have a complicated relationship, but I'm certain that she'll take you in. A day or two at the most. That will give me some time to sort all these things out. You can't go to work and I'll need the keys to your apartment. I'll get you a few things to tide you over. Clothes, toiletries. Those kinds of things."

"Why can't we just go right now? I can just run in and—"

"No." The word felt much sharper than he intended. "I know it doesn't make any sense, and I know you're afraid, but I'm going to ask you to trust me."

Lauren picked up the tented handkerchief off the ground and dabbed at her bloody lips. "Okay."

"Good. What I want you to do is close your eyes and breathe. Just deep breathing while you focus on something that makes you happy. A memory, an object, a place. Anything. Just . . . " He hated himself for what he was about to say. "Just try to stay positive."

William passed through downtown, navigating through the towering spires of the Arcadia District and the deeply shadowed alleyways between them. Alleys littered with mildewed trash and the secret markets and street life of Black Wells' ever-growing homeless population. The clear effect of a boom-cycle mineral economy, both its opulence and its indifference. It was a stain no amount of rain could wash away.

He turned northwest toward the Falcon's Roost subdivision. The part of town meant for the people who worked in the buildings, not those who lived in their shadow. They arrived at 213 Merlin Street just a little after 3 P.M. The rain's heavy drums slowed their beat into a lighter, tap-dancers rhythm. Shafts of sunlight pierced the downy gray in a way that always gave William an uneasy feeling. Rainfall mixed with sunlight gave most people a passing-of-spring-into-summertime feeling. It gave William the willies. He preferred things in an all-or-nothing kind of way. Dark or light. Dead or alive. Clear. Which was absolute hell on a man who spent most of his time dealing with the grayness of the supernatural world.

This little stunt he was about to pull was about as gray as gunmetal. And potentially as dangerous. But a life was at stake, and that was as black and white as it got for him. He parked the car and escorted Lauren to the front door. With a sigh, he knocked.

There was no response.

He knocked again.

Nothing.

"Sarah," he said, knocking harder this time. "It's Will."

From the other side of the door a woman spoke. "You've got a lot of fucking nerve—"

"Listen, I'm not here about that. I've got someone I need you to meet."

Lauren sighed, disbelieving. "Please tell me this isn't an ex-girlfriend's house."

"Like I said, it's complicated." He raised his voice again toward the solid oak door. "Sarah, I've got someone with me."

"I can see that, Will. I've got a peephole. Who's the girl?"

"Look, if you could just open the—"

"I'm Lauren, ma'am. Lauren Saunders."

"Dammit, Will." She let out a sigh heavy enough to pass through the wood. "What's my middle name?"

A smirk of victory wrinkled his cheek. "You never would tell me."

From inside the sound of multiple locks unlatching echoed. The door opened.

Sarah Kestrel wore jeans and a navy sweater; a red and blue tartan shawl mantled her shoulders. The sight of her made his heart ache.

"And I never will," said Sarah, looking them over hard. She flicked her long, black hair over her shoulder and leveled her green, unfair eyes at him. "Spit it out."

He mirrored the look, proving that he was all business. "We need to use the room."

Chapter Five

Lauren

The word that came into Lauren's mind when she saw Sarah Kestrel for the first time was 'fierce'. She was tall and darkly beautiful. Lithe. The shawl-wrapped shoulders angled sharply with muscle. Her skin was like cream freshly poured into coffee, a puzzle of vitiligo that made her green eyes shine like spring leaves swaying in sunlight. While she wasn't the most beautiful woman Lauren had ever seen, she was certainly the most beautiful woman Lauren had ever met. A beauty contrasted by an absolutely filthy mouth.

"You've got to be fucking kidding me," she said, furious. "Four months of goddamn, well, nothing and you show up at my goddamn doorstep with one of your fucking clients who, and no offence, Lauren, I don't fucking know from Eve. And you just tell me that you need to use the room like I'm the cocksucking assistant manager at a Motel 6?"

William put up his hands defensively. "I know it's not the best way I could have—"

"Not the best way you could, what? Come to my home un-fucking-invited and use me like a professional resource? You don't get to do that just because you . . . because you know."

"This isn't about me, Sarah."

"Of course it is. It's always about you or what you need, or what I have that you want."

Lauren cupped her hands in front of her belly and nervously looked around the other houses. Despite the argument, it really was a nice neighborhood.

"All you had to do was pick up a phone and give me a heads-up," Sarah continued. "But that would have taken just a shred of consideration and we both know you're shit at that."

"You're upset," said William in a matter-of-fact tone that even Lauren thought was less than appropriate.

"You fucking *think*?"

William narrowed his eyes in a way that made him look ten years older, and very, very dangerous. "You and I both know you don't have a choice."

"*Fuck. You*, Will."

"Sure, Sarah. Fine. You have to let her use the room, so you can either keep up the Monday afternoon soap-opera melodrama or you can invite Lauren inside and slam the door in my face if you want to. I'm honestly too tired right now to care."

The woman took one, dominant step out her door, bringing herself nose-to-chin with William. "*You're* tired?"

Lauren did not miss these kinds of conversations. She'd suffered through too many of them with Ryan. The two of them stared at each other for what was, maybe, the most awkward ten-second eternity of Lauren's life.

"One, maybe two days. I'll have answers by then."

"You're a real bastard."

"Doesn't change the facts."

"Fine." Sarah turned her furious gaze to Lauren. "I'm sorry for whatever you are going through, honestly. The kitchen is straight back. Wait there. I have something I want to say to Will."

Lauren couldn't imagine what Sarah would need to say

41

privately to the man that she hadn't already broadcast to the entire street.

"I'm really sorry, I didn't know—"

"I know, honey. That's the way he operates. Come in."

Lauren slipped inside the house as Sarah stepped out. She was confronted by a rich, almost overwhelming fragrance of incense. Going the length of the wooden floorboards, Lauren felt like a chided student on her way to the principal's office, staring only at the floor as she made her way to the kitchen, too afraid to look at any one of the interior walls where the three bloated corpses might be standing. The wood gave way to a creamy white tile in what was a quaint, ceramic knick-knack-filled kitchen. A simple, wooden breakfast table rested in a windowed nook overlooking a lovely flower garden in the backyard. Just as she sat down in one of the table chairs, the front door clicked shut, leaving her alone in silence.

Lauren set her elbows on the table and, placing her face in her palms, felt her lips droop into a deep frown. Her body wanted to cry again, but Lauren was tired of crying. Tired of being afraid all the time. Exhausted.

When was the last time she'd slept more than a couple of hours?

During her nursing residency, she worked double shifts in one of South Side Chicago's emergency rooms. That time, though it was mostly a blur, was filled with nightly victims of gang violence, bones broken from overzealous police enforcement, and death. Death and the constant wailing of those who had come in with friends or family that would never see home again. Those months had taken such a toll on her, but it was a rewarding kind of toll. Her job had rewarded her with 'thank you's' from the supplicant lips of those lives she helped save and the smiles of children who sucked with sticky, puckered mouths on lollipops despite fevers or the smell of freshly plastered casts. Even with the little support Ryan gave, he was at least a person that she went home to. It made her realize now that even the smallest crutch helped more than no crutch at all.

Now she was alone. Janet and Sandra had called a few times after the nightclub, sounding worried. Lauren didn't return their calls or text messages, unsure of what to say to them. Then, the calls and texts stopped. Lauren didn't blame them, even though it was Janet who had insisted on Lauren's move to Black Wells. And so, at that moment, but not for the first time in her life, she felt wholly alone. Alone in the kitchen of a complete stranger. The exhaustion made a code-blue-laden night in Chicago appealing. And worse . . . it made her miss Ryan.

Lauren hated when she felt that way, and she felt it more and more often.

The sound of the front door clicking open snapped Lauren out of her thoughts. Sarah Kestrel stepped inside and shut the door behind her. The woman twisted the knobs of what Lauren counted as nine deadbolt locks from the top of the door and so far down that Sarah had to bend at the waist to get the final two.

Sarah turned, put her hands on the curves of her hips and let out a long, frustrated sigh. "That fucking guy," she said. But, when she looked up at Lauren, she wore a surprisingly toothy smile. "Hi," she said, then laughed.

Lauren, for the first time in days, laughed, too. "Hi," replied Lauren, wiping the one tear that had managed to escape.

She walked the length of the hall into the kitchen. "I'm going to have a margarita. Have one . . . or three with me?"

"I haven't eaten in a while, so maybe I shouldn't."

"Well, then, I hope you like steak and potatoes. 'Cause that's pretty much all I eat." The refrigerator was enameled white and looked like it had been pulled out of one of those Fifties' all-American family shows, and when Sarah pulled the chrome handle it opened with the loud, satisfying click of a meat locker.

"What do you say, Lauren Saunders? Steaks and 'ritas sound enticing."

Lauren laughed at herself, wanting to cry again, but this time out of happiness. "That is without question the best idea to pop up in what's been an absolutely terrible day."

"So, what do you do?" asked Sarah as she set out a cluster of potatoes onto the counter.

"I'm a nurse. What about you? What do you do when you aren't cooking for complete strangers who have been dropped on your doorstep like a box of unwanted kittens?"

Sarah laughed, shaking out seasoning onto the freshly sliced potatoes. "It's complicated, but I'm a P.I. of sorts."

"Oh, wow."

Sarah dropped the potatoes into a pot. The oil inside began to sizzle. "Wow?"

"Yeah. Private Investigator is just something I associate with movies. You know, like those old Humphrey Bogart films. My dad and I used to watch them when I was a kid. I guess I never considered that it's an actual thing people do for money."

Sarah grinned wide. "Smart people do *other* things for money. But I'm independently financed by a foundation of sorts. They are my only client. I don't run around and take pictures of cheaters or anything like that. Will tell you anything about me?"

While the potatoes were frying, Sarah made margaritas in a blender.

Lauren waited between pulses of the blender to talk. "Nothing at all, really. Just said you had a complicated relationship. Which, in retrospect, was as mild as he could have put it."

Sarah chuckled, it was almost an angry sound. "Yep. That's William Daniels for you. A real dickhead when it comes to full disclosure." She dipped her finger into the mixture and tasted it. Her expression warmed and she let out a deeply satisfied hum. "Honey, your panties are going to need a seatbelt."

Lauren threw her shoulders against the chair and laughed. She liked Sarah Kestrel.

Sarah poured the both of them a drink, set one next to Lauren, and then went back to check the fries. "But," she shook her head, shifting the conversation back to Will, "to his credit, he did tell me everything about your situation. And for as much as I could have knocked his dick in the dirt for doing what he did today, it was a smart decision to bring you here."

Lauren took a sip from the cool glass in her hand. She blew out a sigh of pure bliss. Sarah had been right, the drink was the perfect mixture of limey tang and sweet tequila heat. "So are you going to tell me what 'the room' is or are you going to give me a William answer on that?"

Sarah took a few steaks out of the fridge and seasoned them with salt. "Absolutely not. You might have guessed from the company I keep that I'm not just a normal private-eye."

"I didn't want to pry. Seeing as you're making my dinner out of the goodness of your heart. It felt a wee-bit forward."

"Lauren, I'm a straight-shooter. There are going to be some things that I can't tell you about me, but this part I can because of your . . . predicament." She threw the steaks into a cast-iron skillet, the hot sear sending up a plume of smoke. The smell pulled on a long string inside Lauren's stomach.

"Because of my job, I have access to certain resources that normal people would find difficult to understand. Just like I'm sure you find it hard to believe that you're being attacked by these strange things that no one else can see, hear, or touch. But, from what has happened to you first-hand, you cannot deny their realness."

"Right," Lauren said, then took a deep drink from her margarita.

"It's good, right?"

Lauren nodded. "Never had better."

"Never will," she said, flipping the steaks. "There are things that exist inside and outside our world that sometimes have direct influence on us. Different mythologies say it all different ways and no one, not me or even Will, can say just how much of it is real and the rest of it is bullshit. I don't typically truck in Will's side of things and very, very few people ever get involved in mine."

"So, he's a real exorcist. Demons and angels and all that?"

"The genuine article." Sarah plated the steaks and fries, grabbed utensils and set the plates down on the table. "Eat while it's hot and the drinks are cold."

Lauren cut into the steak, the savory red juices ran all over the golden-brown potatoes. She ate hungrily.

"My house is engineered to be a kind of barrier between the mundane and weird side of shit," said Sarah after a deep swallow of her drink. "Think of it like a fortress that makes it very difficult for . . . spirits, we'll call them, to get inside. But, for particularly nasty situations, inside this fortress of mine I have a room that doubles down on that protection. That's why you haven't seen those women who've been pestering you the last few months."

Lauren had been about to slide more of the potatoes into her mouth when her hand froze. She hadn't even thought of it until now. The dread that had filled her mind since the night at the club was absent. Like someone had removed a swollen infection by finally plucking out a nasty splinter. The emptiness of where the splinter had been was still there, but there was relief also.

"Just noticed it, huh?" Sarah said, chewing a hunk of her steak.

"It's just so . . . unreal. I can't believe it."

"Honey, sometimes *I* can't believe it, but this shit is as real and constant as death and taxes. Like I said, I don't work in Will's world all that often, but because of our past relationship, he knew my place could protect you. Which, as you can now see, despite my previous flip-out in the yard, I'm happy to do."

Lauren slid her plate away, full and satisfied. "So, who is he? I mean, what does he do?"

"Will?"

"Yeah. Can he really help me?"

Sarah leaned back in her chair, her smile twisting almost mean, but with a gleam of memory. "William Daniels is a single pin-prick of light amid an irrepressible darkness."

Again, Lauren's shoulders hit the back of her chair. "That's . . . a big statement."

"Just wait. In his realm of the weirdness of everything, he's a colossus of occult knowledge bestriding the gap between good and evil, his heels dug into the mundane and supernatural banks. And though I sometimes cannot stand the sight of the man, he is someone who the pantheon of Hell considers one of their most potent foes. Though he pretty much hates God, he remains heaven's champion in a part of the world he thinks the man upstairs has abandoned."

"Abandoned Black Wells?"

"Sure enough. And he has evidence for the theory, too. Even though he's a terrible boyfriend, Will shoulders a crushing weight I can't even imagine. Among the circles of humans in-the-know about the war between the high and the low places, he's a polarizing figure. To say the least."

Sarah took a long drink from her margarita, then continued.

"No one is exactly sure what to do with an excommunicated exorcist. Hell wants his soul and the Church treats him like a kind of holy atom bomb. But they're hesitant to use him because he's a living reminder that even His Holiness in Rome can't speak on all accounts for the Heavenly host. So it's a delicate balance, an ethereal stalemate, when it comes to William Daniels."

"Sounds like you admire him quite a bit," said Lauren, then finished her drink. A warm calm started to pass over her, making her sleepy.

"Do I admire him?" Sarah asked herself, placing a finger to her chin almost mockingly. "It's impossible not to. As an image, Will is a sincere pillar. As a man? Well, let's just say I see the cracks around that sinking foundation."

"Makes sense. I'm guessing that's why he meets with Doctor Irvin."

Sarah cocked an eyebrow. "Huh?"

"My psychiatrist. That's how she knew him. William goes to her for counseling."

Sarah shook her head. "Yet another moment where William Daniels left out a key piece of the story."

Lauren took a long, nervous sip of her margarita. "You didn't know he was seeing a shrink."

"Negative." The woman clenched her jaw. "Well, that's certainly going to be interesting for that doctor of his."

"Yeah. I didn't put it together until the car ride over here that he probably wasn't just a professional acquaintance. I had one of my attacks while I was in her office, so she gave me his information. If she hadn't . . . "

Lauren let it go, not wanting to go down that path of thinking.

"You're tired," said Sarah. "I've got some things I need to take care of, but before I do, I'll get you settled in your room and I'll be back lickety-split."

Despite what Sarah had said about the room being a fortress, Lauren did not like the idea of being alone. "I—"

"Hey, it's okay. Don't be afraid. I wouldn't go if I wasn't absolutely sure that you'd be safe here. And honestly, I don't have a choice. My job isn't one that you can just take a day off."

Lauren's mind, like William had said on the porch, was too tired to argue.

"Come on, let's get you settled. Don't worry about the dishes," said Sarah, standing up.

Sarah took her down one of the hallways of the house into a small bedroom that . . . well, it looked to Lauren just like any other bedroom. There were no magical symbols or weird candle configurations anywhere. Lauren didn't even know why she'd expected that. It was just a simple room with a single bed, made up in blue-and-white checkered sheets, a bedside table, and a lamp. A waist-high bookshelf was stuffed with paperbacks in the corner, too. But at a second glance Lauren did notice a few strange things. There was no closet and no window. No TV.

No pictures.

Not even a mirror.

Lauren was too tired to worry about any of that, though.

"Here's your bunk," said Sarah. "I'm going to ask that you stay in this part of the house, preferably in here until I get back. If you wake up and can't get back to sleep, just avail yourself of one of the many trashy romance novels I inherited from my grandmother. *He Walks In My Garden* is a particularly steamy event if you're up for it. Bathroom is just across the hall if you need a shower or use the can."

"When will you be back?" asked Lauren. She was sure she looked more desperate than she wanted.

Sarah surprised her with a hug. Her strong, sinewy arms gave off tremendous security. "Don't you worry, Lauren. If I'm not back by the time you wake up, just give my cellphone a ring. The number is on the wall next to the phone in the kitchen. If I don't pick up," she said, squeezing Lauren's arm, "don't panic. Call Will. His number is on the list under the scratched-out number . . . which was also his."

"I thought he didn't like phones," said Lauren.

"He's got a cell, he just screens all his fucking calls. If he sees it's from my place, he'll pick up. One-hundred percent. Don't worry," said Sarah, looking deeply into Lauren's eyes, as if to pass along some of her strength. "Oh," she said, dipping her hand into her jeans pocket. "Here are your keys."

"Did Will not need them?"

"He called a taxi. Just in case. But he and I both highly suggest not driving anywhere. Unless it's an emergency."

"Right."

"Like I said, don't worry. Will knows what he's doing. If anyone can help you from here, it's him."

Chapter Six

William

"**I don't have** a clue what I'm looking for, Karl," said William, peering under the open hood of his ancient Mercury Montclair.

Karl Bishop slumped his big shoulders and leaned his considerable weight against the hardtop. "The alternator, Padre. It's right there."

"See, you keep pointing and I keep looking but, alas, your automotive ways remain a mystery."

Karl used the back of his hand to wipe a smudge of grease from the dark wrinkles of his forehead. "This car is a classic. It deserves to be taken care of. But it's all good. The less you know, the more you'll end up paying me."

"I just need to know it won't break down on me again."

"It was manufactured a half-century years ago. If you want reliability, I suggest you sell it to me and get yourself a Honda."

"Just give me the damage."

"Twelve hundred for the parts and labor. I went ahead and replaced the original brakes and installed a set that won't require an empty airstrip to come to a full stop."

"I didn't ask you to replace the brakes."

Karl slapped William on the shoulder. The playful strike stung his arm down to the elbow. "Call it an investment in public safety."

"You'll take a check, of course."

"You know I won't." Karl shut the hood of the car, the heavy metal sent a boom through the shop.

"Do you happen to accept indulgences?"

"That joke will never be funny."

"Fine. I'll hit the bank on my way to the Kasdan."

"Ah," remarked Karl, running a grimy rag between his thick fingers. "Got a client?"

"Yeah. Had dinner plans with Sherry, but I'll have to cancel. Need to get some research in before tomorrow."

"She's not going to like that. But, you do what you gotta do, so long as you're willing to suffer the collateral damage."

William shrugged.

Karl strode behind a high, neatly kept countertop where a 'World's Greatest Daddy' coffee mug sat, its contents black and cold. Next to it were stacks of invoices tucked into plastic sleeves. The mechanic flitted through them until he found one thick as a gambler's money clip. "Anything I can help with?"

"Other than a parts and labor discount?"

Karl looked up, his brow a thundercloud, lightning in his eyes. A brief glimpse into what William knew to be a fierce and oftentimes violent mind.

"No," William replied, back to business. "This one seems purely ethereal. Some kind of haunting or, and I'm hoping this isn't the case, someone finding out that they've got a connection with the other side."

Karl scanned the invoice then walked over to a closed steel door that served as the key room for all the vehicles in the shop. Reaching into his pocket, he produced a little coin. "Well, if you find anything that needs bleeding . . . " he said, flipping the coin in the air.

"Sure," said William.

Karl caught the coin in his palm and slapped it onto the wrist of his other hand. He examined the result. Then, he opened the key room door and shouldered inside.

William admired the garage bay. The sparkling chrome and freshly waxed paint contrasting the black rubber of the tires set on a shop floor clean enough to eat a Christmas dinner off of. The other cars, spangling in the sodium lamps, were works of art, but it was the pearl-white vintage Corvette Stingray that was the prize in Karl's collection. "You got any plans tonight?" he asked.

"Hunting." Karl said, still inside the closet.

"Going back up to the mountain?"

"You know me, a tiger in the snow."

"How is my girlfriend and my goddaughter?"

The metallic clink of Karl flipping his coin rang through the bay. He came out of the closet and shut the door behind him. "See, that was *almost* funny. Keep practicing. Things are fine at home. Carrie and I are busy with work. Leia is reading everything she can get her hands on. Math grades could be better, though."

Karl tossed William's keys over the counter.

They hit the exorcist right in the hands. Flailing in ricochet, the keys collided with Karl's coffee cup. The loop of the handle broke away in a solid "C" shaped-piece. The keys slid over the lip of the counter, slapping the floor.

William cursed.

"Close," said Karl.

"You're kind to suggest so," said William as he swiped the keys up. "Thanks again. I owe you."

"Twelve-hundred dollars, for the car. The cup was a Christmas gift from my daughter, by the way."

"Priceless?"

"You bet."

"Put it on my tab."

William rolled out of the Bishop Automotive parking lot, the big engine of the Montclair rumbling louder than the thunderclouds still lording over the Black Wells skyline. The long, black car carried him on black leather seats that were smooth as wet seal skin. At a red light, he dialed Sherry's number. He explained the situation and Sherry understood, though she kept him on the phone for the entire fifteen-minute drive, making him feel bad about it.

Before making his way to the Kasdan, William returned to his office. Night began to fall, and the cold, gray rain clouds cast spear-thrusting St. Michael in a dark and gloomy light. The spear in his hands might be meant for the Devil . . . or perhaps aimed for the world beneath. God's wrath somehow always found its way toward both.

William lifted the chairs, making sure the rollers were set precisely within the worn dimples rubbed into the wooden floor. A place for everything and everything in its place. He pinched the broken china pieces between his fingers and carefully slid them into a paper bag. The china would never have a place again, but the set had been a gift from Sarah, so he carefully placed the bag on a small, plain desk that still required a secretary. A place for something, no one for the place. One of these days he'd get around to hiring someone. He had the money, but never the time to find the right person to fill the seat. Maybe he'd put 'Fine china repair' in the job requirements section of the classified. That would be weird, but after all, it wasn't like it was a normal secretary position. The person who took up the job would need to be capable of handling the secret strangeness of his business or already have experience on that side of the world.

Occultists didn't retire and get desk jobs though.

No, the fate of an occultist never ends with award ceremony that climaxes with a golden watch and a fat pension. Typically your career in helping people survive demons or vampires or ghosts or *whatever* was usually insanity. Death for the lucky.

It was those thoughts that sent him through the reception area and into his actual office. First he took communion. Then, he took his medication.

Neither was something he wanted to do. Each was preventative. Both necessary.

Despite his displeasure in taking them, he always felt better after he did. Another twelve to fifteen hours of clarity and peace of mind that the things he saw were real. That the voices he heard were from actual people.

There was a little closet in his office where he kept a change of clothes. He skinned off the wet priestly vestments and changed into a navy suit and chestnut brown tie. Fresh socks and brown oxfords later, he felt crisp and awake again in the way that only a pressed suit can make a person feel. He transferred his keys, knife, a rosary looped through a golden ring, and brass lighter to his pockets. Finally, from the closet, he grabbed his umbrella. It had been stupid not to keep it with him, but he'd been at home when the call from Cardinal McMichael had come through and hadn't wasted time to come back to the office before going to the cathedral.

He rifled through the mail, considering each piece carefully, trying to ignore the large, brown envelope. Trying not to look at sweeping calligraphy swished along the envelope in onyx ink.

There was no address written on the envelope. No sender. No stamp.

Just his name.

He sliced the top of the envelope open with the slender, sharp blade of his pocket knife. Poured the contents onto his desk. Three items slid out.

A check for ten thousand dollars.

A second, smaller envelope, sealed with wax.

A slick photograph that fell face down onto the desk. An address written on the back.

"Son of a bitch," he said.

William signed the check and folded it into his jacket pocket. He slid the blade of his knife through the sealed envelope, took out the sheet inside.

He read it.

William, my champion, it began.

He rolled his eyes, then read the rest.

You are needed at the home of Martha and Walter Jacobs. Their daughter, Miranda, is suffering. She is twelve. I am sure that you are pressed by other matters, but I am certain that you will make this your top priority. The Jacobs are desperate, as they have been dealing with Miranda's affliction for two weeks now. A picture of Miranda is enclosed, taken two days ago.

Your monthly stipend is enclosed. As ever, it is to my good fortune that you are mine to call upon,

Forever,

Teresa

William picked up the hefty receiver on his office telephone and dialed Sarah's phone number from memory.

The line rang and rang.

Rang again.

William felt a sinking feeling in the pit of his stomach. Had something happened?

The line picked up with a mechanical click.

"You've reached Kestrel Investigations. I'm out. Leave a message. If this is an emergency . . . sorry." The line beeped.

"Sarah, this message is for Lauren. Let her know that I'm working on her issue, but I've got a stop I need to make. From you know who. Tell Lauren I'll get her things from her apartment and deliver them tonight or tomorrow morning. Call me on my cell when you get this."

He hung up the phone and considered calling back. But he told himself everything was alright. Sarah's house was safe. And should a malevolent force try to get to Lauren, Sarah was the last person they wanted to screw with. He locked up the office and went back to the car.

He coasted around Miller's Hill, a little nature preserve and park set at the center of the Arcadia District. The pearl-

and-silver analog clock set at the center of the Mercury's obscenely long dash read 6:46 P.M. The lamps lining the long, black streets burned phosphorus-white, casting deep shadows across the face of a little, private storefront. The Kasdan Archive was a four-story building that had been built during the art deco phase of Black Wells's architectural movement in the late-thirties. Sherry, of all her many historical passions, often talked at length about how the city had transformed from pioneer town into a place whose architecture rivaled Chicago's late nineteenth century turn toward impressive structures built to stand the test of time.

The Kasdan Archive was a perfect representation of that movement. All four stories were layered to provide a stark, illuminated outline. Rounded, brass arches set on white stone curving at the top into a stained-glass cupola. One might mistake the archive for a federal building and never suspect it was one of the wealthiest repositories for occult knowledge in the world. The architecture was grand and the volumes vast, but it wasn't the books or the bricks that made the Kasdan special.

William parked along the street and approached the great, black mahogany doors. A brass plaque, bolted into white stone, read:

THE KASDAN BUILDING
EST. 1913
PATRONS & PROXIES ONLY

He slipped over to another brass plate, opposite the other, that bore a mother-of-pearl button just above three vertical speaker slots. William pressed the button and waited.

"Name."

"William Daniels."

A bell chimed just behind the doors.

57

William stepped inside, and pulled the door closed behind him. A hollow, metal sound echoed through the cavernous library as tumblers locked back into place. He took off his hat, partly out of habit, but mostly out of reverence. He stood there, scanning the rotunda of bookshelves stretching from marble floor to brass fixtures inlaid into the crown molding. The warm, unmistakable aroma of books greeted him like a friend. Set at the center of the bottom floor was a massive circular desk the color of honeycomb and inside that circle sat the greatest resource within the archive, the repository's sole archivist—Marvin Lockhart Kasdan.

The dark-skinned youth looked over the top of his gold-rimmed glasses and flashed an all-American smile. "Mr. Daniels. Welcome back."

"Marvin," William greeted him, the hollow echoes of his footfalls following him the whole way. "How are you?"

They shook hands.

Marvin turned his hand over, gesturing politely at a gold-leafed ledger on the desk. "If you would be so kind."

William picked up the pen next to the ledger and wrote down the time. Next to that he wrote the word 'Teresa' above the line reading 'Patron'. Then, he signed his name.

Marvin nodded. "The archive is at your disposal. Please, how may I be of assistance?"

William leaned an elbow on the counter and rubbed his brow. "This one is a bit outside my comfort zone. I've got a suspicion as to what it is and I'm hoping you'll be able to tell me I'm wrong about it. " He described Lauren's situation discreetly, leaving out personal details.

Marvin hummed in consideration. "Detrimental communication occurring with increasing regularity. No prior family history with the supernatural or psychosis, at least not that you know of. Recent move to Black Wells. Disassociated from personal trauma. And the forces behind the event are capable of interacting with the tactile world."

"Yep."

"You know I hate speculating . . . "

"I'm pretty sure I know what you're going to say," William said.

"I think you've got yourself a late bloomer, Mr. Daniels."

William rubbed the bridge of his nose. "Shit. You don't think it could be a haunting, something tied to the nightclub?"

"Highly unlikely. You are, of course, familiar with the first book of Samuel and the tale of King Saul's consultation with the Witch of Endor."

"Fuck me," William moaned.

"That's quite the selfish take, wouldn't you say?"

William straightened. "Yeah."

"The Canaanite witch, while absent from some of the earlier versions of the deuterocanonical texts, is one of the key influences in our understanding of not only ancient positions toward witchcraft, but spiritual mediums as an occult phenomenon. Especially the attitudes toward women in that respect. The key feature of the Canaanite's resurrection of Samuel's spirit before Saul is one of the earliest accounts of a medium being unable to control the manifestation they conjure."

"Second floor, then." William rubbed his chin.

"And some of the third, I'm afraid. Might I suggest the works of Conrad von Junzt, specifically. After producing the *Unaussprechlichen Kulten*, he went on to pen a lesser-known pamphlet entitled *Die Graue Welt*."

"My German is a bit rusty—"

"Roughly translated *The Gray World*. A marvelous little book detailing von Junzt's time at a Romani encampment that produced a shocking number of psychically hypersensitive women. These women, he recounts, did not simply interact with the supernatural forces, but commanded them. There could be something

59

in there for your client; perhaps something that might help her control these . . . attacks as you called them. Shall I put the coffee on for you, sir?"

"I've got another appointment that I need to see about first."

"Ah."

"Look, can you do me a solid and put together all the volumes you think might be useful? I'll be back later tonight, or maybe tomorrow morning."

"It would be my pleasure," he said, nodding politely.

They shook hands again.

William made his way outside. Night's veil had fully fallen, both the sun and the rain gave way to a cold, gray darkness. The burning glow of the street lamps stretched along slate sidewalks and slick, black streets. He dipped into the Mercury, twisted the key in the ignition, turned the heater up full blast. When his fingers were warm enough to grip the steering wheel, he angled the car south toward the home of Martha and Walter Jacobs.

Chapter Seven

Lauren

Lauren slept deeply for the first time in months. Her dreams were strange. Surreal. Beginning with Lauren following the swishing tail of Maxie, a yellow tabby cat she'd grown up with. Maxie meowed softly at the back door of a house Lauren did not recognize, but somehow identified as her home. Lauren opened the door, the cat slinked outside into a palatial garden-style backyard. In the midnight gloom, amid the cold darkness Lauren spotted a glowing pair of eyes. Eyes that were fixed on her.

Afraid, Lauren turned on the back porch light. There was a strange shape loping in the darkness, and suddenly, into the light came a large, black-and-white tiger. It lunged for Maxie. The tabby cat tried to dart away, but the tiger caught her with one swiping paw, bringing her into a crushing grip while the tiger slowly began to tear the cat apart as if the flesh were made of taffy. Where the tabi's fur peeled away revealing a flat, crimson sheen of writhing muscle.

Maxie keened, her little claws and fangs doing nothing to the beast while it, without much effort, peeled the cat apart.

The last thing Lauren remembered was screaming and running toward the tiger. But when she stepped off the lip of the front porch she fell down into the grass, which was not grass at all, but a thick, mossy liquid into which she sank. Lauren tried to swim, but her arms refused to move. Her legs became as heavy and immobile as stone.

Lauren sank into the green, feeling her lungs start to fill up with mucus-thick fluid. Her hearing drowned out to the sound of Maxie's dying.

She came screaming out of the nightmare slathered in sweat. A familiar, acrid smell hit her nose immediately. What was normally the sharp tinge that came from a patient's bedpan wafted from the sheets of the bed. Her underwear and thighs were damp, burned raw from the acidic properties of her urine.

"Did I . . . " she asked to the empty room.

She knew she had. The embarrassment of the accident made her feel very young and somehow vulnerable. Her throat was dry again, almost raw. Her forehead felt tight and heavy with a lingering headache. Even worse was the bloated pressure she felt in her stomach. No doubt the effect of the quickly-eaten steak and tequila-rich margarita.

Lauren thought about calling for Sarah, but stopped short, not wanting the woman to find her laying there like a frightened child in the soiled bed. She got up, stripped the covers, thankfully finding that the mattress was covered in a plastic fitted sheet. With the damp sheets and wet plastic bundled in her arms, Lauren went into the bathroom. She flicked on the light, tossed the bundle into the shower and turned on the hot water.

She peered into the hallway. Dark and quiet except for a single pillar of light cutting a hard line through the hallway from the kitchen. Lauren listened for footsteps.

Nothing.

The bathroom's quaintness matched the rest of the house. The white tile floor was cool on her feet. Black, diamond-shaped tiles lined the perimeter of the room. Downy, golden towels embroidered with white, jasmine flowers flanked a porcelain sink. Above that, in a mirror, Lauren's tired, sunken face stared back at her. She stripped down and threw her wet clothes into the shower as well. Just as they hit the water, she realized that she didn't have a spare change of clothes. Unless William had brought her things while she was sleeping, she was going to be up shit's creek without a paddle.

Closing the bathroom door, she let out a sigh of relief. Hanging on a sterling hook was a downy, gray bathrobe. She slid the laundry pile to the back of the tub and stepped in.

A sigh of carnal pleasure passed over her lips. The shower spray was hot and clean. Though the jets stung the skin between her thighs at first, that feeling subsided, sliding towards absolutely heavenly. The clear stream washed away the sweat of her nightmare and the rest. The clean heat of the water rinsed her body and her fatigue. She let the water slap against her tongue, taking a mouthful to gargle the dryness of her throat away. Pitter-pattering on the lids of her closed eyes, soaking her hair, cascading down her back; the hot shower might have been the greatest invention in the history of mankind. The very pinnacle of civilized life epitomized in this one, simple device.

Lauren lowered the angle of the showerhead and sat down. When the water began to lose its heat she resigned herself to bathe. Again, the skin of her thighs burned when she lathered them with soap, but that chemical sting subsided once the water cleared the bubbles away.

The towel next to the bathrobe felt soft and smooth, warm on her skin. She dried herself and wrapped the towel around her wet hair. She slipped the robe over her shoulders, sliding into it like a fluffy blanket. Above the sink she smeared her hand across the fog-veiled mirror.

In that palm's width of clear, reflective glass Lauren stared again at the woman gazing back. Could this really be her? The heavy bags under her eyes, the normally round, perky cheeks sagging. The lines of her frowning face formed the old, familiar mask of a woman who had spent days pulling shift after shift in the ER. A mask of exhaustion and sorrow that foretold the theft of youth and beauty. Flesh, mind, and heart, all of them drawn the full length of their endurance.

Back in her room, she picked up her cellphone from the nightstand. 11:41 P.M. She'd slept for five hours, wishing she'd made it all the way through the night. Going through the long, dark hallway, she found Sarah's washing machine inside a closet. The laundry went in easy enough, and if this little string of luck kept going, she might be able dry the sheets and have them back on before Sarah even got back.

Hadn't she said she would only be gone a couple of hours?

Lauren remembered Sarah telling her to call if she needed anything. But, did she really need anything? She had the situation under control. Lauren would hate to interrupt her if the P.I. was in the middle of something important. She stepped into the living room to see if William had dropped off her things, but there was no sign he had. The furniture stood, dimly illuminated by the light coming from the kitchen.

Throat still raw and stringed with dried mucus, probably from dehydration from Sarah's margaritas, Lauren got a glass of water in the kitchen. Sarah and Lauren's unfinished meals were next to the sink. She ate a few soggy fries off her plate. Still hungry when those were finished, she picked up the remaining steak between her fingers and tore off a cold hunk of meat. She swallowed, but the meat scratched her throat so badly she winced trying to get it down.

Lauren gagged.

She cleared her throat.

When she tried to inhale, nothing happened.

Her raw throat seized up. She couldn't swallow.

Couldn't breathe.

Reflexively, against everything she had been taught to do as a nurse, she reached her fingers into her mouth, probing her throat to pull out the mass lodged in her airway. Her lungs burned and she broke a sweat. Her jaw opened wide and tears welled in her eyes. She tried to hack a cough, but though her stomach heaved, the blockage refused to loosen.

She gagged again, her mouth filling with hot saliva.

Lauren dropped the glass and it shattered in the sink. A gray fog floated across her vision, but she saw the wooden chairs next to the table. She placed the knuckle of her thumb deep into her diaphragm, then dropped her weight down onto the shoulders of the chair.

Air whistled through her throat, passing around the stringy edges of the meat. Spit now drooling over trembling lips, she smashed into the chair, harder. Still, the mass didn't budge. Stamping her feet, furious and teary-eyed Lauren rocked back on her heels, swayed to the tips of her toes, and jumped, leaning forward with all her weight. The impact was blinding.

The gray, chewed mass flew out of her mouth, slapping against the seat of the chair. Lauren inhaled, sucking in air so deeply that an animalistic sound she did not recognize as her own came out of her. Her stomach churned and, leaning over the edge of the chair, she vomited. It was the most violent spasm she had ever known. Bile and regurgitated pulp splattered against the chair, sprayed the floor. She felt the relief of pressure from her stomach immediately.

She wiped her mouth to clear away the strings of spittle over her chin, but when she did, something strange wrapped around her palm.

Lauren opened her eyes.

Her dripping mouth widened, not with the desire to vomit, but in stark disbelief at what she saw on the chair, all over the floor, and hanging from her fingers. It was a thin humus of moss. Not mucus. Not remnants of food.

Black bile and thick, green moss.

Lauren shot up, scrambling to the kitchen phone. She looked at the number written below a series of angry black strokes. Her fingers hurried over the numbers.

Lauren stamped her feet in place impatiently. Her heart thundered, her breath panicked by desperation nearing hyperventilation. The chiming ring on the other end of the line jingled and jingled over and over.

"Pick up the phone, you son of a bitch!"

The ringing stopped.

"Hello? William?!"

No voice replied. Only the buzz of static—no, not static. It was a slow, gentle sound. Like the sound of a wave sloshing against stone.

Lauren jammed the receiver harder against her ear. "William, are you there? It's Lauren, please say something!"

"Lauren." It was a woman's voice.

"Lauren." Another woman.

And a third. "Lauren."

Something intertwined into Lauren's hair, then twisted, curling the strands into a knot. She cried out, jerking the receiver away. Whatever held the knot of her hair coiled tighter, angry, crushing the hard receiver into the flesh of her ear.

"There are faceless children with countless sins." The three voices spoke now as one. "Sins countless."

Lauren screamed. Again she tried to pull the receiver away from her ear, using both hands. The strands of hair painfully ripped free from their roots. "Let go!"

"Find the faceless master," the trio of voices spoke. "For the punishment of faceless sins."

Finally, with one, hard yank, Lauren tore the phone free. And just for a moment, out of the corner of her eye, the receiver was not a receiver.

It was a bloated hand of ghostly white flesh, black-nailed, veined in cold, blue blood.

Lauren threw the phone and, screaming, ran down the hall back toward the bedroom. She slammed the door shut, slapping her palms against the door, afraid that something might come after her and pound its way into the safe space. That is what Sarah had called it—safe.

The moans coming from her mouth were the trembling sobs of shock. Eyes squished shut like a child hiding under their covers from a monster seen in the crack of an open closet, Lauren ran her hands down the surface of the door. Then she turned and slid down its length. The wood was rough and cold.

Cold as stone.

Her fingertips trembled over something slick and hard. From somewhere across the room, Lauren heard the sliding of feet and the slow, gentle drip of water falling upon rock.

"W-What do y-you want from m-m—"

The sound of approaching steps chewed into her ears. Grinding into her skull.

"P-please."

The rancid odor of death accosted Lauren's senses, emanating not an inch from her nose.

Cold skin slid over Lauren's cheek, sliding wetly to curl her hair around her ear.

Lauren made no effort to pull away, she was frozen. Sucking each breath through quivering lips. "What do you want from me?" The words a soft, desperate whisper.

Three voices answered her in slow, cold succession.

"Let."

"Us."

"In."

67

Chapter Eight

William

The Mercury jumped on its shocks, popping the curb running alongside 5831 Milner Drive. William cursed, rolling the huge steering wheel to the left so that the tire grinded back into the street. He grabbed his black medical bag and hurried up the darkened driveway through the singular shaft of lamplight slanted against the front door. He rang the doorbell.

Muffled voices rumbled behind the door. One of them lilting in a question he could not make out, then it was repeated louder.

"Who are you?"

"I'm William Daniels," he said calmly, trying his best to give off a professional tone. "I am here about your daughter."

A worried series of interrogative tones later, the door opened a little. Between the links of a taut chain-length, a man's face appeared. "Are you the priest?"

"I am not a priest, Mr. Jacobs. But I am someone who can help you with your daughter's current malady. Now, may I please come in? Of the few factors that determine success, time is the most important."

"Let him *in*, Walter." A woman's voice came from somewhere behind the door.

The stern, protective gaze Walter Jacobs gave William

belied the dark circles of fatigue under his eyes. "I am going to let you in. Don't make me regret it, or *you* certainly will."

"I understand."

The door clicked shut, the privacy chain slid away, and the door opened fully ajar. Standing just over the threshold was a hunched, slender man of middle age and height. Just to his right was a woman, taller than her husband by a head, with thin blonde hair draped over her wide shoulders—Martha Jacobs, William surmised. She placed a hand on Walter's shoulder, saying, "Please, won't you come in, Mr. Daniels."

William stepped into the house, removing his hat.

Walter closed the door behind him and they stood in the little foyer together.

"I have a few questions and then I will get right to work," said William. "Firstly, I understand that whatever has occurred here over the last few weeks has been difficult and painful. I have been doing this kind of work for a very long time—and, I assure you, Mr. and Mrs. Jacobs, I am very, very good at my job."

"And what job is that precisely?" asked Walter.

"I am an independent consultant employed by someone who learned of your daughter's situation. That person employs me to handle these kinds of afflictions with a careful hand and discreet manner. Now, my questions."

"Go ahead," said Martha, her thick arms crossed over a pale nightgown.

"Are you Catholic?"

"No."

"I don't see how—"

"When did you notice changes in Miranda's behavior?"

"A little over two weeks ago," Walter said, "We found her in the backyard where she was . . . messing with a few dead birds."

"Messing?"

"Mutilating," said Martha, her fingers caging her lips. "She was mutilating them."

"And that mutilation turned into acts of self-harm, yes?"

Walter's brow wrinkled. "Y-Yes."

William hummed in consideration. "And when did Miranda first attack you, Mrs. Jacobs?"

Martha's eyes widened as she looked over at her husband. "A few days ago. Maybe Tuesday. How did you know?"

"It's my job to know. Now, have you seen any kind of behavior that may not be categorized as natural? Furniture moving, feats of improbable strength or the recitation of knowledge that would otherwise seem impossible? Speaking in different languages. Anything like that?"

Martha opened her mouth to say something, but Walter gave her a look.

"Time," said William. "The more I have, the better Miranda's chances are. So out with it."

"She mocked us about certain . . . ah, intimate details about our sex life that there is no way she could know about."

"No objects moving, as if tossed or shifted by an unseen hand?"

"No."

"Is Miranda restrained in the room?"

"Like, tied down?" asked Martha. "No."

"Okay. And has the voice she spoke with always been her own, or has it changed? Has she said any names you don't recognize?"

The parents shook their heads.

A loud bang resounded from deep within the house. Martha jumped and Walter's head snapped to look down the long hallway.

"Please focus," said William, bordering on impatience.

"But—"

"Have either of you made any kind of compromise or deal with your daughter since she began showing signs?"

70

"What do you mean?" Walter said, looking back at William.

"Did Miranda promise you that things would go back to normal if you did something?"

"Y-yes. She said if we sat in a circle with her and prayed, that it would make everything better."

William nodded, trying to hide the stone of worry that fell into stomach. He took a step to his left, ensuring that his back was no longer against the door. "And did you engage in this prayer?"

"No."

"Mr. Jacobs—"

Martha butted in. "We sat down together, yes, but the prayer she wanted us to recite was . . . " Her voice caught in her throat. "It was horrible. We both left the room without speaking a word of it."

William scanned their eyes for a moment. When he was satisfied that they were telling him the truth, he said, "I am going to go into Miranda's room. Once I go in, you cannot enter. You may hear things that lead you to believe that I am harming your daughter, but I assure you, my hands will never touch her. The thing hurting Miranda will want you to believe that I'm causing her harm. I assure you that will not be the case. So, you *must* not enter the room. Is that clear?"

The Jacobs nodded silently.

"All three of us have the same goal—to help Miranda."

"We understand," said Martha.

"Good. Now, if I could please trouble you for a cup of water and, if the smell coming from the kitchen proves accurate, a fresh cup of coffee."

Martha led them into the kitchen where she gave William both a mug of coffee and a glass of water. William took the coffee, but asked the woman if she could pour the water into a plastic vessel. He didn't need anything flying across the room that could hurt him, should the entity within have some form of telekinesis. He'd known a colleague who'd lost an eye after making that mistake.

"Please, wait in the kitchen." He gestured at their little, wooden four-top. "This could take some time." William lifted his palm to face them. With his other hand, he extracted his pen from his pocket. "And please, no matter what you hear, do *not* enter the room until you've seen me again. If I do not come out within an hour you are to call this number," he said, writing a number down on a notepad, then placed it on the kitchen counter.

He blew on the coffee and drank it in three swallows, then set it on a decorative shelf filled with family photos. Miranda was smiling in all of them. Playing. Hugging her mother, cheek to cheek. Jumping off a high-dive into a pool.

The last one made him smile.

A smile that quickly fell into a deep frown.

"Shouldn't we pray together or something?" asked Walter.

William turned to him, reflexively narrowing his gaze. "Why?"

"I dunno. That's just what I thought priests do."

"Like I said, Mr. Jacobs. I'm not a priest. Which room is she in?"

"Umm, the last door on the left," said Martha.

William walked the length of the hall, the plastic cup in one hand and his bag in the other. The last door on the left was littered with crayon drawings. Fields of flowers with four stick figures standing in the yellow blossoms. Another was of a red river running through a mountain valley. Hanging from a thread of blue yarn from the doorknob was a rectangle of yellow construction paper. Written on the sign in blue marker was:

Miranda's Friendship Club!!!

Boyz need not applie, Daddy allowed tho

There was no light coming from under the door.

William inhaled deeply and rubbed his tired eyes. He let out the breath slowly.

He opened the door. It swung open smoothly, the knob banging slightly against the wall.

The sharp odor of human waste slapped him in the face, an aroma that had become a professional acquaintance.

Gloomy moonlight slanted through the slats of wooden blinds set across the room's lone window. The window was set directly above a mess of tattered sheets roughly clawed to ribbons. A yellow-painted dresser squatted against the left wall. Little golden figurines balanced atop marble pillars, each of them kicking a soccer ball in one fashion or another. The floor was cluttered with de-limbed dolls and slumped piles of clothes. A soccer ball that had been ripped open lay next the wrinkled laundry like the sun-rotted rind of a peeled fruit. To the right of the room was a little writing desk and a half-open closet door that shielded the inside from where he stood.

William set the cup of water on the bedroom carpet.

He stepped out. Shut the door.

Again he took a deep breath, thought about the layout of the room, putting together all of the pieces he had seen. To himself he said three sentences. A practiced mantra that he knew by heart, but never failed to recite.

"Demons lie."

He took out his pipe.

"Demons cheat," he said, filling the pipe with tobacco.

A scuttling sound came from within the room, near the door. Then it receded.

He snapped open his lighter and brought its flame to the bowl of the pipe. "Demons can be cast out." He sucked the stem of the pipe, the flame bent down into the bowl, flashing the tobacco to life.

The doorknob turned, squealing with age. The door cried on its hinge, opening to reveal the same darkened bedroom as before. This time, William stepped inside and closed the door.

The moonlight caught the curls of smoke, drifting over to where the closet door was now pulled closed.

William sat on the small child's bed. He unsnapped the top of the bag open and set it next to him.

A hushed voice sliced though the flat darkness between closet door and frame.

"I was thirsty and you gave me something to drink." It was the voice of a little girl, high-pitched and happy.

William pulled on his pipe. "I was a stranger and you invited me in."

The girl giggled inside the closet, her laughter dripping in a low baritone. "Miranda isn't feeling well."

"She is sick, yes. And in a prison, so I have come to visit her."

A small set of fingers slid through the gap of the frame, curling around the bottom corner of the closet door. Slowly, it opened. "And what is your name, priest? Tell me yours and I will tell you mine."

Demons lie.

"Father," he said.

"Oh." It was a long, drawn-out sound. "Father is a title. Not a name, priest." The low voice hissed the last word like a snake.

Demons cheat.

The exorcist blew out a long, curling jet of smoke.

"Faust," he said.

The door came fully ajar, creaking on its hinges. Sitting cross-legged, clothed in a soiled pair of flowery pajamas, the creature inside of Miranda gazed with a pallid stare out of the girl's eyes. Her lips drew back, flashing angry.

"*You*," it said.

"Yeah, motherfucker," William said. "*Me*."

Chapter Nine

Legion

We are **Legion.**
Out of many, one.
From the time of the Great Divine Schism we have freely roamed within the broad, red line of violence that began with Cain and shall never end unto the end of ends. We bear a perfect memory of a journey traveled among thrilling atrocities past and see dimly the feast of wars to come. We have watched thousands of heart-freezing winters and locust-swallowed harvests, a trillion heartbreaks from summer loves and the drowning spring floods spilling over homes since the first waters split void and form. Pillaging fires and blood-soaked rape, to our cheers, done in the virtue of conquest.

We are the snarer.

We are Legion.

Out of one, many. Many that cherish one common delight, one delicacy that never spoils despite the many, many years of our indulgence. Like moth to flame or death to the pestilence tent, we are the one of many who rapture not in the screams of war or in the last whisper of breath belched from the parched throats of the deprived.

Many sins are palate-pleasing, but only one sates the hunger of the demoniac.

The suffering of little children.

I'm afraid.

A little voice whispers from within our darkness. Tiny Miranda, worthy of admiration, morsel-sized. Though a mere mortal morsel, her flavor is greater than a banquet of adult sufferings. We will say nothing to her. Give her only darkness. For what do children suffer more greatly than the dark? Her fear nourishes us; drives away perfect love. Love, the wretched barrier that banishes perfect fear. Love that warms the human heart to wretched hope. Hope that we salt with long-suffering.

Miranda's suffering will last until every succulent, marrow-deep drop is drawn from the well of her soul. And leaving behind the dried, mortal husk, we will go out and seek another.

We are Legion.

Many hungry threshers, scything to one harvest.

Can anyone hear me?

The silence seasons the fear, but we are not cruel. We will end the lonely quiet by speaking to her in many voices of one accord. We will say, "No one can hear you, precious Miranda. No one will ever hear you again."

But not yet.

For while captive Miranda cries out, hidden within our shadow, there sits before us a bane. A spoiler of feasts, uninvited and unwanted.

"You," we say to him. We have heard his name. Know his works.

He mistakes our hatred for fear.

We are Legion. We *are* fear.

He calls us violators of matrons in primitive idiom. This Faust, strengthened from the High Place, has grown proud with his cheap victories over the lesser of our kind. He does not know the depth of our darkness. Does not know the hollow ache of the ravenous.

What he does not understand could fill a cosmos of

cosmoses. What he does not see would render a prophet blind. His trinkets are impotent. His belief infirm.

We, the many made one, stood before the heavenly Host ITSELF! And though HE cast us out and sent us among the swine, we persisted. We, the one made many, survived the GOD-MAN. Of what do we fear from just a man?

"Where is Miranda?" he asks us, despite knowing.

Who is that? I can hear you!

A portion of our number grip her by the arms of her soul's construct, casting our weight upon her like many chains. And with the tiniest fraction of our strength, we cast Miranda into a darker place. A deeper pit.

"I want to talk to Miranda," Faust commands.

We crawl toward him, from out of the little closet space, and sit innocently—ready for war. Miranda's voice comes from our lips. "I do not suffer the commands of a fool."

Though we have peered into the eyes of many, those set before us are different. Their colors are offset, strange in their proportion and temerity. There we see the apostle's confidence and the frenzy of the prophet's apocalypse-vision. He smokes slowly, confident that it will not be a future cancer that destroys him.

"Fine," he says, leaning closer to us. "Who are you?"

"Call me Polyphemus, Hellbane."

"And who am I to you?"

"No one."

He sighs, a liar's gesture. We can see truth in those eyes.

He enjoys this game.

"You know who I am. The quicker you tell me your name, the quicker we can get this over with. One way or the other, your eviction papers are here and I've got other shit to do."

His vanity, like so many others of his church sworn ilk,

swirls about him like a shield. But with this one there is no aura of the divine about him. No holy light. We see in him a pale reflection of our own darkness. All save for the eyes, the ice and the jade. How does he hide his faith from us? In what cleft of his soul does he hide the candle of belief?

He is intriguing to us. Almost playful. This puzzle of a man leans closer.

"Give me your name, I command you."

We laugh. Our work is almost complete and this man, this *thing*, utters at us commands without any heavenly authority. One might as well try to snuff out a star with a whisper. Demand the oceans to deliver the mysteries of their deeps. The human tongue has no such authority.

"No," we say. "You are too late, Hellbane. In mere minutes this vessel will yield to my will. And then we will be outside even your cursed reach.

He shakes his head, perturbed. "Goddamn you."

We smell the air. In it is the closeness of victory. We hear Miranda's little voice from the low place. Her will is almost eclipsed.

And yet . . . something is amiss. Wrong. Though we are old and many, the exorcist's eyes shift amid his smoke. Open wider. Moonlight slices across them, revealing not Hell's black lake or Heaven's golden sheen.

For only the second time in our long-lived primacy, we recoil . . . a hog's squeal escapes our many mouths as one sound.

The thing shaped as the man opens wide, splits somehow, penetrating our shadow not with light, but a greater void. And dear Master of Hell's own fire, we are drawn forth like Leviathan on a hook. We are drawn out of Miranda, our form sliding past her teeth, over her lips. Yanked into the harsh miasma of reality, we sear against the pale moonlight. For millennia we have hunted as unseen oppressors, invisible to the eye of every mortal man and, even some, of the angel-kin. But as we are sucked out of delicious, little Miranda, we turn our many sets of eyes into Faust's.

He can see us.

A man without fear.

We see.

We are deceived. This man is no mere priest. Nor exorcist.

Faust is a prison.

And the last thing we see, just before we are pulled into a darkness we cannot call our own, is the smile of the exorcist.

A prismatic burst of light sears us.

Hurts us.

Jails us.

We are Legion.

We are made many prisoners to occupy one cell. And though we smash our many hands against red walls of an unknown prison, one new truth is revealed to us.

We cannot get out.

Chapter Ten

William

There **was an** uncertain amount of time that passed once the ritual was completed. Exhausted and crowned in sweat, William blinked his way back into the world. Miranda's little form lay in a crumpled heap near the closet. He breathed in the smoke from his pipe, letting the heat caress the bottom of his lungs. Then, he exhaled. Reaching over, he scooped up Miranda, carrying the little girl to her bed. There was a coolness to the girl's skin that distressed him. When he set her down, he quickly drew back at what he saw.

Miranda's skin was blue as moonlight, and her face . . .

Her face was not the face of the girl in the kitchen photographs. It was the face of an old woman, weathered and wrinkled. What flowed out from her skull was not hair but silver-white strands that glimmered in the light of the moon. Her lips were the blue of deep water.

Whatever he had set on the bed, it bore no likeness to that of a child.

"What the—"

He blinked.

There lay Miranda. A skinny girl with the pink skin of youth and slender lips. She breathed softly, letting out a little moan as she rolled over, tugging her comforter over her shoulder.

William shook his head and rubbed a hand over his tired face.

He remembered taking his medication.

Or was that yesterday?

No. The pills came first and then came communion in his office.

How long had he been here?

Pulling his cellphone out of his pocket he checked the time, but where there should have been a digital clock, there was only a thick yellow band running across the screen.

8 Missed Calls—Sarah Kestrel

7 New Messages—Sarah Kestrel

15 Unread Text Messages

William cursed, slid the phone into his pocket and gathered his things.

He opened the door, stopped. Looked back at Miranda Jacobs, then hurried into the hall back toward the kitchen.

The Jacobs were in the hallway. Walter was leaning against the wall. Martha, sullen-faced, sat with her knees pulled up to her chest. When she saw William, she braced herself against the wall and rose.

William stood there, looking at them.

"Well?!" snapped Walter Jacobs.

"I—"

"Is she going to be okay?" asked Martha.

William shook his head again, and took a deep breath.

"Miranda is going to be okay. She should start therapy as soon as possible."

"You're sure she—"

"I am sure," said William. "Listen, I have an emergency and have to go. Call that number I gave you, they will provide you the number for a therapist who I trust."

Martha Jacobs threw her arms around Walter's neck. The woman trembled there, her weight of her fear and her exhaustion cast fully upon the husband.

Walter looked over his sobbing wife at William. "Thank you. I don't know—"

"It's my job, Mr. Jacobs," he said, pushing past the two of them toward the front door.

William slid behind the wheel of the Mercury. The clock read 1:48 A.M. He dialed Sarah's number.

Sarah answered. "*It better fucking be you, Will.*"

"It's me. What happened?"

"Did you not listen to any of my fucking voicemails or read my texts?"

"Just tell me what happened."

In the background of Sarah's apartment William heard a woman scream.

"Get your ass over here and I mean right fucking quick."

"I *am*. Now," he said, cranking the engine to life, "is Lauren okay?"

"No, Will. Lauren is not *fucking* okay. Something got through."

William's heart fell into his stomach. "What! How?"

"I don't know *how*, but it did. And . . ." Lauren's scream boomed over the line again. There was a tremor in Sarah's voice, an uncertainness that William had never heard before. Maybe, weakness. "Whatever it is, it's outside of my expertise."

"Where is Lauren?" he said, roaring into the street. "Why isn't she in the room?"

"Like I said in my billion texts and voicemails, Will. She *is in the room*. And the room isn't doing shit!"

"I'm twenty minutes away. But I'm hurrying."

"You damn well better."

William hung up the phone and tossed it onto the passenger seat. He refused the desire to slam his foot on the gas. Getting pulled over would be the cherry on top of what had been a terrible twenty-four . . .

He took a breath. Then, rewound the day in his mind.

In the last twenty-four hours he had performed two exorcisms, one of which he was forced to trap the demon inside himself. Watched a woman get physically assaulted by an unknown entity or entities. Get into a fight with his foul-mouthed, stunning ex, who now was housing his client inside an unbreachable magic room that had been impossibly breached. All while hallucinating that the victim of the second exorcism was somehow made of ice. On top of that, he still needed to get back to the Kasdan Archive and research ways to help what might be Lauren's latent psychic ability that had revealed itself because . . . well, Black Wells. And he'd driven all over the city in a vehicle that he still owed twelve hundred dollars for the repairs on.

When was the last time he'd slept? Or eaten?

Had he taken his medication? Taken communion?

The latter two had to be true, because the ritual with the demon inside of Miranda had worked like a charm. That success gave him a charge of confidence, but that wouldn't carry him much further.

It was moments like this in his life that William believed that God or Black Wells was actively trying to kill him. Sometimes he wondered if they were the same thing.

William drove as fast as he could, edging over the speed limit through the mostly empty Black Wells streets, arriving at Sarah's house 11 minutes after 2 A.M. He scrambled out the car, clipping his foot on the lip of the curb. He fell, catching his weight with his hands. The gravel cut into his palms, but he pushed himself to his feet and slammed the car door. A few bounding strides brought him to the porch. He lifted his hand, but the door swung open before it could land.

Sarah stood there, a red gash bleeding above one squinted eye.

"Christ, Sarah. Did Lauren attack you?"

"What? Oh, no," she replied, pointing to the gash. "Work-related."

From inside the house there came a harrowing scream.

"Well," said Sarah as she pivoted on her heel to give William open access to the door. "Get in there, Slugger."

William half-stumbled down the hallway, almost cratering the drywall to keep himself upright. Just before he pushed open the door, he called back at Sarah, who was following him. "Get your record player and your vinyls!"

"Huh? Why my—"

Lauren screamed again, wailing a painful moan.

"Just *do it*, Sarah!"

William grabbed the doorknob. The brass handle was cold. So cold that it seared the flesh of his palm. He reflexively pulled back. The cold sphere refused to let go of his skin, ripping patches of skin from his already scuffed palm and fingers.

William sucked a breath through his teeth.

Lauren stopped screaming.

The house fell silent.

Mad as hell, William said, "Fuck this supernatural cold bullshit." And kicked the door just below the knob; it buckled but refused to open. He kicked again, this time harder. The door flew open, banging against the wall.

The light was on.

Lauren stood in the far corner of the room, facing the wall. There was a white bathrobe crumpled at her heels. Her naked flesh was slick with condensation and her auburn hair was dripping, matted against the middle of her back in one thick tendril. William stepped inside, the cold snatched him by the throat. When he managed to exhale, his breath passed over his lips in a white vaporous plume. The doorknob had been searingly cold, but inside the room was a different kind of cold. Still. Quiet cold. The kind of cold one might find in the arctic. The cold that renders a land barren. Cold that cut William to the marrow.

"Lauren," said William, his teeth already chattering.

Sarah rushing, stumbled. Catching her weight on the

wall, she then tried to barrel into the room. William stopped her with an upraised palm.

"Is this you?" he asked Sarah, referencing the freezing temperature.

"No," Sarah replied, her breath hurried. "I've got the—"

"Plug it in. Put on Mozart."

"Are you serious?!"

William lowered his voice barely above a whisper. "The Sull'aria. And when it starts, don't move."

William looked back at Lauren, waiting.

Lauren trembled. Her slender fingers curled around her arms, hugging herself.

The record player hissed to life in the hallway. The needle fell on the album, scratching into static. Strings hummed to life. Then, there came the voice of a woman, bright and gentle, meandering into the silence. The soprano's song rose and fell with the dreamy, carefree grace of a flower petal dancing on the wind.

William closed his eyes, listening, focusing. He waited until another soprano joined the first, their dissonance twisting into harmony, two petals fluttering against each other. The sopranos swallowed the silence. Swallowed the world. And, then, what William had hoped for finally happened.

The voices swallowed the cold. The permafrost lining walls and bookshelf steamed into vapor. The deathly chill lifted from the room.

"Lauren," said William, approaching her from behind.

"No," she said, but it was not Lauren's voice. It was a strange sound, like several voices speaking together. A community of voices like he'd just heard out of Miranda Jacobs. But, somehow different.

"Do you hear the music, Lauren?"

Lauren inched closer to the wall. "Tired," the voices said. "Cold. Lied to."

"Will," said Sarah. "Did you bring a possessed person into my house?"

85

William, keeping his focus on Lauren, shot an angry, upraised index finger back at Sarah while keeping his eyes on Lauren.

"I will not lie to you," he said. "You are tired. Rest. I will get you a blanket to warm you." William, again without looking at her, opened his hand toward Sarah. Silently gesturing for her to get a blanket.

Lauren snapped her head to the left, showing William one of her blue eyes. "All lie."

"I tell you the truth, if you rest, I will help you."

"The liar," said the trio of voices over the duet of sopranos coming close to the end of the song. "Punish the liar."

William had to get her into the bed before the music stopped.

"I will hear you, but first lie down. Drift to sleep."

Then, slowly, Lauren turned away from the wall to face the bed. She took a slow step.

The sopranos came into their final stanza.

"Good," said William, his voice was gentle and calm.

Lauren slid onto the mattress. "We are still cold."

The soprano's final notes rose high, coming to a peaceful crescendo.

Sarah dropped a blanket in William's open hand. He took it and approached Lauren.

"Rest," he said, covering the blanket over the woman's damp flesh.

The duet finished, leaving only the quiet hiss of static. Sarah lifted the needle.

William dropped down to one knee and placed his palm against Lauren's forehead.

"Shit," said Sarah, exhausted. "What the hell was that?"

William inhaled slow and deep, then let it out with a tired shudder.

"That," he said, looking at Sarah, "was a cry for help from the other side."

They were sitting at the kitchen table when Sarah asked, "How long do you think she'll be out?" She hooked a curved needle through the flesh just above her eyebrow, stitching together the gash.

William looked down into the steaming, black cup of coffee in his hands. "Should be a while. The sedative I gave her should keep her under for six or so hours."

"The music was a nice touch. Never heard of that before."

"Music soothes the spirit."

Sarah pulled a section of stitching shut. "You didn't know it would work."

"Worked for King Saul. I had a pretty good idea it would work for her."

"You're the worst damn liar I know. It's why you tell half-truths instead."

"I compartmentalize."

"Compartmentalize. You get that from your shrink?"

William looked up at her, annoyed.

"Lauren let it slip. Relax, I think it's good for you. Just wish you would have told me sooner."

"My business."

"How long?"

"A while."

"While we were together?"

He sipped the coffee.

"That's what I thought. See, something like that would have been *our* business."

William set the cup down, silent.

"What's going on with you? You look more tired than I've ever seen you and that's saying something. You cut off all communication months ago, right after you went to Buffalo. What happened?"

"You know, for someone who said that her work required absolute secrecy, you sure don't mind probing other people's business."

"Everyone has secrets. I'm required to keep certain things from people. It's my job. I think, after your vanishing act, I deserve a little better than that."

"Tell you what," he said, relaxing. "You let me make myself a steak and tell me how you got that," he said, pointing at the gash she was almost finished suturing, "and I'll tell you all about what happened in Buffalo."

Sarah turned away, considering. She looked at the clock. "Christ, it's three in the morning. Let's get a bandage on your hand. We'll talk over breakfast tomorrow. If Lauren wakes up first, you'll at least be rested for that. But yeah, we'll talk."

"Mind if I take the couch? I'm not in a condition to drive."

"Sure."

Sarah bandaged his hand quickly and efficiently. Then, she brought him a couple of blankets and a pillow where he stood in the living room. William slid off his coat and loosened his tie, resting them over the back of one of the leather chairs.

"Thanks," he said.

Sarah laughed to herself. "No problem."

William watched her thin, strong fingers make the couch into a bed. He admired the black and white flesh swirling on her skin. She turned and their eyes met.

"I am sorry, Sarah." His voice was tired, deeper than normal. "I really am. For everything."

She shrugged. "What's happened has happened. And for what it's worth, I'm proud of what you're doing for Lauren. I've always been proud of your work."

He imagined wrapping his arms around her. Like they had before. Leaning his cares into her warmth. "Sarah, I—"

"Goodnight, Will."

She'd seen it in his eyes and rejected it outright.

"Goodnight, Sarah."

She walked out of the room, never turning back. Never once smiling.

He lay down on the couch, examining the bandage bound around his hand. He let it fall onto his chest, where he felt his own heart beat against it.

Chapter Eleven

Lauren

In the depth of her dreaming, Lauren stepped barefooted upon a field of marigolds bathed in buttery sunlight. The sky was cloudless and blue. A mountain rose up before her, a deeper shade than the sky, capped with snow. A cardinal song fluted through the wind, coming from a conifer-laden glen sloping toward a ribbon of water that flowed down from the mountain. Purple waters emanating from the downy-white mountain tops charged, white-capped, down the west facing stone.

Standing near a white-fanged curve of the river was a woman and a child. It looked like a boy with dirty blonde hair, no older than four or five. Lauren called out to them but, when she tried to speak, she found she had no voice. The woman was shorter than Lauren, but slender, dark-haired, and even from this distance Lauren could see the woman's smile.

She was laughing.

The little boy with her was laughing, too.

Lauren walked toward them, watching them clasp hands. There, next to the purpling river, they began to spin. Spin so fast that the momentum lifted the boy's feet from the ground. They twirled and danced and laughed, unaware of Lauren's approach. The woman lifted the boy into her arms. His spindly legs wrapped around her waist.

Lauren called out again, though her words made no sound. An observer only, she found herself pulled closer by the gravity of their happiness. They spoke.

"When will Dad get here?" the little boy said, leaning back.

"Sometime soon, I think," the woman said. She kissed the boy on the nose.

He wiped the kiss away, giggling. "Will you spin me again?"

"*Again?*"

"Yeah, do it again. Spin me until Dad gets here!"

"Honey, Mommy is so tired."

"Please?"

The woman turned only a quarter-circle, then said, "There. Happy?"

The little boy shook his head, still smiling. "Nuh-uh!"

"*Fine,*" the woman said, her exasperation comically overplayed.

And they spun again, around and around in the marigold field, the woman's feet splashing in river shallows.

When the woman came around, she stopped in mid-spin and looked directly at Lauren.

Uncertainty passed over the woman, her smile faded from her scarlet lips.

Lauren stopped, arrested by the woman's quick emotional pivot from joy to anxiety.

"Have you seen my husband?" she asked.

The boy, held in his mother's arms and facing away from Lauren, said, "Who is she, Mommy?"

"She's no one, sweetie."

"She must be someone," he replied. "Do you think she's seen Dad?"

The woman asked again, "Have you seen my husband?"

Lauren shook her head.

The woman's smile returned, wider than before. And she stared at Lauren for a long, long time. So long, remaining still. So still, it took Lauren almost a minute to realize that while the woman's dress was swaying in the wind, her eyes didn't move. They just stared at Lauren. Unmoving. Unblinking.

"Liar," the woman said.

The word snapped through the air like a sharp pair of scissors snipping the strings of a marionette puppet, Lauren without understanding, lost her ability to stand. She fell into a tangled heap among the marigolds. Immobile. Her legs had folded under her, each foot turned at awkward angles. Her arms were powerless, though she could feel her shoulders holding their weight. Though the angles and immobility unsettled her, the realization that she could not hold her head up sent a cold sweat down her spine. With the way Lauren's paralyzed neck bent under the weight of her skull, her chin was pushing against her own esophagus, pinching her windpipe shut.

She tried opening her mouth to breathe.

Her jaw didn't move. It remained pressed against the top of her sternum.

Lauren's nostrils felt so narrow and incapable. The harder she tried to inhale the less she seemed to take into her lungs. Her stomach churned. The pressure in her chest was like someone sitting directly on her, refusing to get up. She wheezed. Her vision grayed at the edges.

And then, out of the corner of her eye, Lauren saw the woman stepping through the flowers. She placed a bare, wet foot on Lauren's shoulder and shoved her over.

The fall didn't hurt. And the marigolds felt soft against Lauren's face. The sunlight was still warm. The cardinal's song continued.

Lauren could breathe again. It was such a simple, biological mechanism. In and out. Inflate, deflate. This wasn't like choking in Sarah's kitchen. The panic that had come over her was that of slow inevitability, while the steak lodged in her throat had been acute and immediate. Lauren had existed as a severe asthmatic for only a few moments. Known the fear for less than a minute. There was an indescribable relief of an open airway, and Lauren had known it once in reality and now, even in her dreams.

"Please," said Lauren, her voice finally making a sound. "Please, help me."

The marigold stalks lengthened, growing higher until they were the only thing Lauren could see. They bent in the light of the sun, wrapping around Lauren.

"Where is she going, Mommy?" the little boy asked.

"Oh, she's going to the place all people go, Sol," the mother said, walking away. "Into the ground."

The stalks of the marigolds coiled tight around Lauren's neck, burning her skin, constricting her throat.

"He—"

The marigolds silenced Lauren, sending their flowers into her mouth, through her teeth. Over her tongue. Down her throat.

Lauren tried to bite the stalks, but her teeth were not sharp enough. The flowers crawled down her esophagus, so deep that she could feel them slither into her digestive tract, expanding her diaphragm, and writhe in her stomach like worms. And slowly, maddeningly slow, the marigolds swallowed her into the earth.

Mother and son continued to spin near the bank of the river, laughing over the muted sound of Lauren's screams.

Chapter Twelve

William

Dawn reddened the living room curtains, waking William. The grumbling hiss of percolating coffee dripped down the hallway from the kitchen. His stomach growled angrily as he rolled off the couch.

Lauren was still sleeping.

Good.

In the kitchen, Sarah leaned over the counter on her elbows, watching the coffee drip. She was wearing plaid pajamas and a white tank top. The dark hair she normally let hang over her shoulders was wrangled into a ponytail. All along her shoulders, lean biceps and forearms were bright, purple lines and red-blue starburst of fresh bruises.

"Morning," she said, her voice hoarse.

Above her eyebrow, a massive bruise the color of a plum encircled the red line of her stitches. During their time together Sarah had come home roughed up a few times, but nothing like this. Her muscles, which were normally taut and lithe, sagged with fatigue.

"What the hell happened to you last night?" asked William.

"Can I at least get my coffee before you start the whole grand inquisition thing on me?"

William didn't press the issue. "Sleep well?"

"Like a rock. You?"

"Not bad. Checked on Lauren. She's still out."

"Good for her. I've got an appointment at one. I'd appreciate it if the two of you were out by then."

"Sure."

"Thank you." She sighed. "I like Lauren, but I can't have her in my place while I'm not here."

"Not even if I stay with her?"

"And you were doing so well," she said, reaching up to grab a mug from the cabinet. "I don't want *either* of you here while I'm not. If she's going to keep experiencing these episodes, she can do them at your place. If that room can't protect her from whatever it is she's got going on, then there's no reason for her to be here. I've got too much shit going on to have to worry about that, too. It isn't personal . . . at least not with her."

Sarah poured William a cup, then one for herself. "Still in the mood for a steak?"

William took the cup from her. "Absolutely."

She walked around him to sit at the table. "You know where they are. I'll take mine with a couple of eggs."

"Fair enough."

"And while you're busy not overcooking my breakfast, you can spill it about Buffalo."

"I know how you like them," he said, grabbing the carton of eggs from the fridge. "It's a long story."

"Like I said, I'm not out the door until after lunch."

William cooked their breakfast in silence, gathering his thoughts. The sizzling of the eggs seemed to prompt the end of Sarah's patience. She practically barked at him. "Well?"

"It goes back further than Buffalo," he said, scooping the food onto plates. He went over to the table and sat down. He passed Sarah her plate and sawed into his steak, beginning. "About seven years ago, I was ordered to perform an exorcism here in Black Wells. This was before the Church let me go. Before that, I spent most of my time traveling the world at the behest of His Holiness. Places like China, Morocco, Nigeria, but lots of places here in the States, too."

"So, seven years ago . . . "

"Right. There was a family who had a son, well, *has* a son as far as I know, possessed. Not your run-of-the-mill oppressor, either. One of the bad ones. Duke of Hell kinda thing."

"Of course," she said, sliding a bite into her mouth. "Of course they have a hierarchy."

"Even in Hell there's a pecking order. The boy, we'll call him Jonathan, was exhibiting major signs of possession: speaking in languages he didn't know, moving things through sheer will, communicating with people through their thoughts, temperature manipulation."

"So . . . *The Exorcist*-type shit."

"In every piece of fiction there is a sliver of dark truth. The difference here is that it's real. There isn't the vomiting or pea soup. But there is pressure. A malevolence that affects every sense. Ever been in a dark room or hallway and suddenly feel like you were about to be chased?

"Who hasn't?"

"It's like that, but all the time during the exorcism. Even inside a fully lit room. Your fight or flight mode is constantly engaged, sometimes hours on end. Makes the whole thing exhausting."

"So, Jonathan's going all Linda Blair?"

"In spades. The Papacy sent an exorcist in before me—Father Nolan. Nolan was one of the best of us. Even trained in the same monastery and had the same teacher as I did. I know for a fact he'd assisted in dozens of cases and never, not once, had he failed to emancipate the victim."

"Except this one," Sarah said over the lip of her cup.

"Jonathan's mothers, when they hadn't heard any sound from the room for a few hours, went to check on the priest and their boy. They found Nolan, dead on the ground. He'd choked to death on his silk stole."

"Stole?"

"You've seen mine. It's the silk band I wear around my shoulders. It's supposed to work like a mantle of protection, a holy barrier that guards the priest from demonic attack. The mothers were horrified. They found Jonathan sitting in his bed, innocent as a lamb. He looks at them and says, 'He was thirsty, so I gave him something to drink.'"

"Fuck."

William nodded. "So, I get the call from the Holy See himself to get my ass to Black Wells. My words, not his."

"They didn't send anyone else with you?"

"Exorcists are specialists. There aren't that many of us. And the Church still holds the pretty arrogant position of 'one possession, one priest'. I had a good record at the time and with . . . certain situations surrounding my previous life before my training, they thought I would be capable enough to handle it. They even sent me in with a holy relic—a silver communion chalice blessed by Pope Leo IX." William paused, remembering the details clearly of a living nightmare he would never forget.

"Will?"

William shook his head slowly. "Two weeks. I was in that house twenty hours a day for two weeks. Trying to discern a way to learn the oppressor's name. Getting the name means I can command it to leave the victim."

"Sure, I get it."

"I tried everything. Roman Ritual, invocation of the Host, and even a risky technique of trying to trade the demon for its true name, while also letting it believe that I would give it mine. And therein is the danger. Demons lie. Always. Except in the moments when they believe a truth can lead to a greater lie."

"I'm guessing the road works both ways with names," said Sarah.

"Right. With my name on its lips, the demon could do to me what it did to Father Nolan."

"Didn't work?"

William ignored the question. "On the thirteenth night, I was at the limits of myself. And more and more I felt the weight of the oppressor about to swallow up Jonathan for good. So, as a last resort, I . . . "

Could he tell her this?

What would Sarah think?

"Will?" she asked.

"I would never let a demon take a child from the world, Sarah. I would do anything to prevent that. And so, I made a deal."

Sarah rubbed the bridge of her nose, sighing. "You made a deal with a demon?"

"I did. I would allow the demon to have my true name if it swore on its own name that it would leave Jonathan and invade a different host, anyone else living within Black Wells. If I could not find the new victim, the demon would get to keep my true name and still have a victim. Jonathan, however, would be emancipated and we would all live to fight another day."

William took a deep breath, leaning toward Sarah. "Now, I know that demons lie and I know that demons cheat. And what would be more enticing to a demon than to possess an exorcist. But what the demon didn't expect is that *I would lie*. That *I* would cheat, too. And . . . this only worked because the demon didn't know that I . . . "

Sarah searched his eyes. "You?"

"The demon didn't know that I had previously experienced possession myself. And I knew how long it would take before the demon could take full control of my mind."

"Wait a minute," said Sarah, putting up her hands. "You were fucking possessed *before* all of this?"

"I was. Long time ago."

Sarah set her palms flat on the table and leaned forward. She let out a long, slow breath.

"So, I gave it my true name, and as I suspected the oppressor flowed out of Jonathan and throttled my soul immediately. With what remained of my own will, I took the blessed chalice of Pope Leo, which I had filled with my own blood, and a blessed section of the Eucharist. I invoked the holy rite of communion in an effort to send the demon back to Hell."

William paused again to sip his coffee.

"And?!"

"That experiment did not yield the results I expected. The rite of communion didn't export the demon to Hell. What it did was turn my mind . . . my soul, into a prison."

"You're telling me that . . . right now, inside you, there is a Duke of Hell?"

William nodded solemnly. "And more. For the last seven years, when I have been unable to exorcise a demon, or if I'm running out of time, I can draw a demon out of their victims like lancing a boil. Their influence is shuttered away so long as I continue to take communion. That barrier makes them mostly quiet prisoners."

"That's why you were excommunicated," Sarah said slowly, as if she'd finally assembled a puzzle after finding the last piece.

"Correct. Corrupting the holy rite of communion has been considered grounds for immediate excommunication for over five hundred years."

"Will," Sarah said, clearly trying to remain calm. "That is absolutely insa—wait—you said they 'mostly remain quiet'."

William crossed his arms, leaned his shoulders against the chair. "Around four months ago, I started experiencing auditory hallucinations after my case in Buffalo went . . . rather poorly. I got the job done, but people got hurt in the process. I didn't hurt them, but I certainly wasn't innocent of what happened. But I knew that, when I got back, I had to cut out most of the people from my life to make sure they wouldn't get hurt, too. I also started seeing my psychiatrist, who has me on a low-grade antipsychotic that I take every day, along with communion."

William leaned forward. "That's why I stopped calling."

"Jesus Christ on a crutch. We dated for almost a year, Will. Why the hell didn't you tell me?"

"Sarah, the only things I know about you are that you're from Ohio, you are a magic practitioner, you hog the sheets, and that some nights you come home looking like you went ten rounds in a cage."

"Fair," she said.

"And now, it's your turn to tell me why."

"No."

William felt his brow furrow deeply. "What?"

"Ex-girlfriends lie, too."

His lips curled back, soured by her words. "I—"

"You left," she said, snapping the last word off sharply. "I deserved to know why. Now, I do and I hate what's happened to you. I had real feelings for you, feelings that I hadn't felt for someone in a long time. But you left. I didn't leave you. So in my book, that means I don't owe you shit."

So many emotions rushed through him. He felt shame more than his anger, shame because no matter how angry he got at how Sarah said it, she was right. And there came over him a moment when he thought maybe, just maybe he would tell her *why* she was right. Finally tell her the reason he ran to solitude when he should have run to her.

She didn't give him the chance.

"Leave. Take the whipped pup with you," Sarah said, coldly.

"Whipped pup?" From the hall, William heard the meek, tired voice of Lauren Saunders. She stood in the kitchen doorway wrapped in Sarah Kestrel's bathrobe. The look on her face was one of absolute betrayal. "A whipped pup," she repeated.

Sarah put up her hands. "No, Lauren. That's not what I—Look, I was angry at Will. Not—"

"But a whipped pup? I was attacked. And have *been* under attack for . . . I can't *fucking* remember how long because I can't sleep. And when I do I'm having nightmares that involve me dying horribly or vomiting up weird shit."

Lauren opened her mouth wide, her eyes searching the room with wandering panic. "I don't *deserve this*!"

Sarah said nothing, her eyes wandering the floor, a rare uncertainty there.

Lauren looked at Will, her shoulders sagging both in fatigue and a little relief, he hoped. "My clothes are in the dryer. I'm going to get them, and then we can go."

"I'll be ready," he replied.

When she disappeared back down the hallway, William looked back to Sarah. The proud investigator was looking at her empty plate, shaking her head.

"I—"

"Get out," she said, her rage flaring. "You ever put me in this position again, I swear on your holy Christ that I'll make you regret it."

Chapter Thirteen

Lauren

The walk out of Sarah Kestrel's house was a short series of silent events all tied together with a taut line of tension. Lauren got dressed. Will stood at the door, waiting. No one said anything.

Lauren and William went to the car. Got in.

"For what it's worth," he began, then cranked the engine to life, "I'm sorry."

"It's whatever," was all she could say.

He nodded. "We've got several places to visit. But we'll head over to your apartment first, let you get a few overnight things. I have an extra bedroom you can use at my place. It won't provide the kind of protection that Sarah's house does—"

"Yeah . . . some protection. Really saved the day."

He sighed.

Lauren shook her head, still fuming.

"After today, I'm going to have a lot more information on how we can help you," he said. "But again, you'll be with me the whole time."

When they exited the subdivision, Lauren said, "So, you trap demons inside your mind . . . That's pretty freaking weird."

William laughed at that; it was a strange, wheezy noise. "A nurse and an eavesdropper, huh?"

Lauren smiled.

"Don't worry about it. I should have told Sarah about it a long time ago. She deserved to know."

Lauren mulled the idea over in her mind. The absolute insanity of what a statement like that meant in the living world. "Are you afraid they'll ever get out? Or, maybe, influence you?"

"Terrified," he said, watching the road.

"Mr. Daniels—"

"You know my deepest, darkest secret, Lauren. I think it officially gives you a license to call me Will."

"Do you think that your ability can trap a ghost . . . maybe three?"

William angled the car into a parking space in front of Lauren's apartment complex. "I don't quite think it works like that. But if it does, yours will be the first set of spirits I lock up and throw away the key. Come on, let's get your slumber party gear."

Lauren's place was simple and sparse. A couch, a flat-screen TV, and a recliner purchased at a consignment shop were the only furniture she owned, aside from the bed and dresser in her room. Work and partying with Janet and Sandra had left little time to make her apartment into a home. She hadn't even put out the scented candles she'd bought, so the place still had the stale aroma that clings to temporary living spaces. Moving boxes were everywhere, mostly filled with clothes, holiday decorations, and family pictures, stacked against the far wall of the living room.

"I haven't really had the time to move in properly," she said apologetically.

"It's a nice place. I see the potential."

"It'll just take me a minute to get my stuff."

William walked toward the boxes, examining the words scrawled on them. "Sure. I'll stay here. And if you see anything or feel anything that feels off, you just call out and I'll come running."

Lauren stepped into the kitchen, which led to her darkened bedroom. She stalled in the doorway, then turned back to look at the tall, gaunt man who stood with his hands in his pockets, scanning the apartment politely. "Can you just . . . could you come with me while I get my stuff?" she asked.

He smiled at her. "No problem."

Lauren mindlessly packed clothes into her suitcase and gathered up her toiletries. As she stuffed her contact solution into a bag, she asked a question that had been on her mind since leaving Sarah's house. "Why am I not seeing those women all the time?"

Will lifted one of the blinds with an index finger, letting a slender shaft of light splash against his face. "Spirits might be eternal beings, but it still takes effort for them to manifest. They spent a lot of energy getting through whatever it is that makes Sarah's place special. And they took over your physical form, putting you in that trance. Takes a lot of juice to do one of things, and a whole hell of a lot more to do both."

She looked up at him, hopeful. "So they're all spent up? Like, they've gone away?"

"Not for good, sorry to say. It's more like they're recharging their batteries. Whenever they are strong enough, my guess is they'll come back."

"Oh."

"That's why we're trying to wrap this situation today, or at the latest, over the next few days. But like I said, Lauren, I'm not going to let anything happen to you. We're going to beat this."

"How?"

"The only way people can accomplish anything . . . " The exorcist looked at the ground, as if he were scanning every beige fiber with his full concentration. His voice was low and sincere as he said, "Together."

Lauren's shoulders, which she only now realized were

tense, relaxed. The genuineness of the man's words cut through her fear and fatigue. "You're a really good priest, Will," she said, meaning it.

"Ex-priest," he said, a wry smile creasing his mouth.

Lauren finished packing her things and William insisted that he carry them down to his car. When they were on the road again, William asked her a strange question. "Do you know what a medium is?"

Lauren thought for a moment. "You mean like Whoopi Goldberg in *Ghost*?"

"Do what now?"

"Yeah," Lauren said, sliding one leg up into the seat to face him. "*Ghost*. It's this movie where Patrick Swayze is killed by some banker who is also his friend, so Swayze becomes a ghost and communicates through Whoopi Goldberg's character, who is a con-woman, but also someone who finds out that she can actually talk to ghosts. Whoopi helps him talk to Demi Moore, who was his girlfriend, and that way he can finally say goodbye to her. It's one of my favorite movies."

William rocked back against his seat, surprised. "Huh. Okay."

"What about it?"

"Well, I think you might be a Whoopi Goldberg."

"What!?"

"I'm taking you to a place where I can learn more. The severity of your situation, the sheer kind of influence these spirits have over you when they come calling, it's an absolute tell-tale sign of mediumship. And I don't mean the kind that has a 900 number. You've probably had some inkling of it when you were a kid, even if you can't remember it now. Imaginary friends, conversations with people in your dreams, stuff like that. When puberty hits, the scale usually tips one way or the other, either the gift flourishes or it withers away."

Lauren frowned. "I wouldn't call it a gift."

"Most people wouldn't. The ledger of mediums is filled with name after name of the people who either repressed their link to the other side completely or went insane. But," he said, as he wheeled the car into a parking spot along the street, "that ledger is also filled with the names of men and women who were able to bring healing to the wandering souls who find themselves lost after death. Without mediums, those souls would remain aimless and tortured. Unrevenged."

Lauren shook her head, looking out the window at the plumes of steam swirling out of the storm drains lining the bright, cold street. "Why me? Why now?"

"No one knows why they are chosen for anything, Lauren. Some of them believe it's to serve a higher calling, others think it a curse. The difference between the two is how they perceive themselves. Personally, I believe mediums exist as a part of the supernatural world's . . . let's call it immune system. Mediums can see and hear things the rest of the mortal world can't. Which means they can respond to that communication of spiritual unwellness. Without someone taking action to alleviate the malice and sorrow and pain spirits feel, the psychic energy of that misery builds up. Causing a kind of spiritual sickness. Someone or someplace gets sick for long enough and it becomes haunted. Hauntings are very dangerous because they allow the supernatural to affect the natural; spirits, in their pain, lash out and hurt people. A medium can sense that sickness *before* a haunting takes root. As for why now?" He sighed, rubbing his brow. "That's probably due to your move to Black Wells."

"I don't understand."

"Black Wells is a special place, Lauren. Especially when it comes to the supernatural side of the world. I don't know why." He paused, considering. "Hell, no one knows why. But this city acts as a kind of magnet for spirits and demons, angels and other things even I don't understand.

106

And I say that as an authority on supernatural things. Most of what is supernatural about this place is mostly hidden from plain view. It's like looking at a dark, mossy stream. 99% of people see just the water. .9% of the last 1% can sense the danger in the water, but can't see what it is. And then there's the lucky group that's left over. The ones that look at the river and see the eyes of a crocodile floating toward everyone else. See where it's headed. Because a medium never sees the predator the first time, the attack is always devastating. Like it was for you. And once you see it, Lauren, once you've been taken down into the darkness by that monster, even if you survive, there is no going back to the way things were before it happened."

The rain fell, plunking along the Mercury, where it sizzled to vapor on the car's hot hood.

"I'm guessing that means just moving won't change anything."

"Sorry, Dorothy Gale. This tornado is a one-way trip to Oz."

"So what am I supposed to do?"

"*We*," he emphasized, with a smile.

Lauren tried to smile back. "What are *we* supposed to do?"

"We do what billions of people have done for the last 200 years when they had a problem they didn't understand." He leaned over, and pointed out the window on Lauren's side of the car. "We go to the library."

The building he pointed to was a four-story structure that reminded Lauren of the old noir films she remembered watching with her father. Movies that involved old New York or Chicago. A white stone building with golden arches terminating into a royal blue dome of twinkling glass. It was strange to not have noticed such an incredible architecture when they pulled up, but it wasn't until William pointed directly at it that she saw its grand edifice.

"Come on," he said, opening his door. "I want to show you something."

Lauren and William crossed the busy street, leaping over a large puddle. William stepped to a brass panel riveted into the stone and pressed a pearl-buttoned intercom.

A slender voice came over the comm. "Name?"

"William Daniels."

The door buzzed and William opened the door for Lauren.

Lauren took three steps inside before she stopped, arrested by an incredible sight. To call this place a library was a dramatic understatement. All four stories were lined floor-to-ceiling with what might have been tens of thousands of books. She looked through two, pure glass floors above them, where the building terminated into one solid piece of blue glass forming the dome. This wasn't a library. This was a repository . . . a temple.

The bottom floor, perfectly cut from large sections of marble, ran the entire length of the building. At the center of the bottom floor was a large, circular wooden desk. Carven into the desk were little figures, but she didn't know who or what they were depicting. Standing within the perfect circle of wood was a slight, black man. His smooth, bald head shone as brightly as the golden rims of his glasses in the yellow light of the library lamps. As she walked with William toward the desk, she caught the faint aroma of mint and jasmine.

"Mister Daniels," the man said, leaning over one of the many volumes stacked neatly on the desk next to a steaming tea cup. He looked up, surprised, lifting an eyebrow. "And guest."

"Marvin Kasdan," said William. "Let me introduce Lauren."

"Lauren Sa—"

Marvin lifted a hand courteously, silencing her. "Mr.

Daniels, do I need to remind you again of playing loosely with the rules of the archive?"

"She's going to stay in the lobby. That's within the rules."

Marvin smiled at William. "Technically, yes. However, you know it is proper decorum to call ahead and let the archivist know that a guest should be expected. You have not provided me with that courtesy, Mr. Daniels. And thus, I am woefully unprepared."

William smiled, attempting to ease the tension. "We shouldn't be long."

"And still," said Marvin, his tone professional, if not slightly perturbed. "Woefully unprepared."

"Did you manage to get those books for me?"

"They are waiting for you in the reading room on the third floor. Lauren," he said. "Please forgive my curtness with our mutual friend, he can sometimes be selective with the information he likes to provide, even when it leads to embarrassment for others."

"That's what I hear," said Lauren, finally relaxing in light of the man's calm demeanor.

"The seats you passed in the lobby are available to you, ma'am. Would you care for tea, coffee? Perhaps something stronger?"

"Do you have any more of that mint tea?" Lauren nodded toward the tea cup on Marvin's desk.

"Certainly," he said with a little bow. "Mr. Daniels, if you would please sign in."

William picked up a pen and scribbled into a ledger. "Coffee for me, Marvin."

"Surely. However, as another professional courtesy, I am obliged to let you know that there is another occupant on the third floor. So I will ask you to please obey the rules. We wouldn't want there to be any kind of . . . misunderstanding."

"Certainly," William said, that wry smile returning to

his lips. He then turned to Lauren. "Listen, I should only be a little bit. If you start to feel anything . . . " He spied over to Marvin, who stood sentinel and erect behind the desk. "Anything weird, like before, I want you to close your eyes and start singing 'Ninety-nine Bottles of Beer'."

Lauren chuckled.

William didn't smile.

"You're serious?"

"Keep your mind on something inane. Something simple. And remember, that if you need me, just ask Marvin and he'll come get me."

"I can't go with you?" Lauren asked, a quiet desperation in her voice.

Marvin shook his head. "I'm afraid not. Mr. Daniels current situation denies him that privilege."

"What did you do?" asked Lauren.

"No time for that," he said. "You have a seat and I'll be back before you know it."

As William turned away, Lauren reflexively grabbed his elbow.

"Read quickly, okay?" she said.

William nodded and headed for the stairs.

"Mr. Daniels is a quick reader," said Marvin, a kind of reassuring, almost grandfatherly lilt in his young voice, as he flipped open a section of the desk so that he could pass through. He stepped close to her and tilted his head, playfully submissive. With a flourish of his hand, he gestured toward the chairs in the lobby. "Now, let's see about that tea."

Chapter Fourteen

William

William **Daniels often** thought of what the word 'home' meant. As he ascended the steps toward the reading room, he thought about that word. Rolled it over in his mind. Was home the place where you were born and grew up? Was it the place where one made a family? Was it whatever came in the life after?

He didn't know.

Rounding one of the iron balustrades, his shoes squeaking on the glass floor, he thought about the word and wondered if he would ever have a home again. The scattered boxes littering Lauren's apartment reminded him of his own move to Black Wells. It felt like a lifetime ago. Seeing her apartment in that state put upon him a shoulder-sagging sense of loneliness. Brought to mind how long it had been since he had shared a house with someone. Shared a life.

He was certain he would never share one again. And so, even though surrounded by one of the most beautiful places he had ever been, his heart descended into flat, gray aloneness. The place inside his mind that he shared with dozens of unwanted occupants. How long would they remain his to bear? That he also didn't know.

What the exorcist did know was that there was a person counting on his ability to focus the considerable

111

weight of his experience on giving her back control over her life. William had made a promise to Lauren. And stepping through a doorway into the third-story reading room of the Kasdan Archive he centered his mind on the job. On the work.

The room was simple—yellow carpet, a red desk, and a black leather chair. A little lamp slanted light onto the desk next to a stack of leather-bound books. A white set of gloves were laid there, too, accompanied by a set of reading tweezers next to them.

William wrapped his jacket around the shoulders of the chair, rolled up his sleeves, and loosened his rumpled tie. He slipped the gloves on easily enough, and slid the first volume from the top of the stack.

He took a deep breath. Closed his eyes.

When he opened them again, his mind was sharp, focused. He blurred through the basics of mediumship. That much he knew already. He refreshed his memory on the various manifestations, of which Lauren had many. Clairvoyance, clairaudience, clairalience, clairgustance. Seeing, hearing, smelling, and tasting. All tell-tale signs of clear and present interaction with the other side. These were the common manifestations for some mediums. To have just one of these manifestations was rare. To have four . . . it was almost unheard of. That, coupled with Lauren's ability to manifest an object from her trance, the moss she'd thrown up, put her in a class all her own.

All of the volumes agreed upon this: that while a person might 'experience' the other side, they could not interact with it.

All of them.

All except *Die Graue Welt*.

The Gray World manuscript was a thin, simple thing. More of a long pamphlet than a book. The moldering volume was unreadable to him, but one section had been painfully transcribed from the original German into

English by Marvin's sharp, fastidious hand. As ever, the archivist had proved true to his word. It was through the clear, swooping handwritten translation that William read of a gyrovague priest of pagan tradition who, on a cold September night, wandered into the warm firelight of a Romani troupe. Very little was known about Conrad von Junzt, the author of *The Gray World*, but what was clear from his writings was that he held a deep and uncommonly clear understanding of the supernatural. There was a clarity to his categorization. Detailed simplicity so well-penned, that a marvelous writing style survived translation from German into English, grabbing both the reader's intellect and imagination.

William found himself drawn into the swooping, black ink of Marvin's erudite handwriting. Pulled forth with such ease that the words themselves became pictures in his mind. And those pictures of the man were clear, though the translation bore no description or imagery of the Gyrovagi monk. But the exorcist could see him clearly, see him traveling from wagon to wagon, learning about the women who, from within their little, wheeled homes, could by way of esoteric meditation leave the warmth and safety of their corporeal forms, only to step out into the Gray World. The other side. An incorporeal landscape that von Junzt described with such awful accuracy that William envisioned himself there.

The monk's writing, while it remained clear, seemed to meander on exactly what that landscape looked like so as to focus on what it felt like. For each Romani woman experienced the other side with wild variety. Odors, sensations, the sounds and the sights were diverse in how they might be experienced by each Romani medium. But, what was the same for each of them—what remained consistent—was the color. The spirit world was gray; the gray of an overcast sky lorded over by a black star. A sun forever set in an eclipse casting no light. And it was in that gray existence that the Romani women described not only occupants, but structures that chilled the blood of the occult veteran reading the translation. Towers of variegated bone and flesh mortared in blood. Towers that went on and on, miles high, set against the cold, gray horizon.

There was an order to the gray world. Not just a wide landscape of immigrant souls without a spiritual shore to make their harbor, but a world lashed together in belted flesh and dusty bones, where gray rivers of blood lapped gray corpse-filled banks. The smell of sulfur and decay assaulted the nostrils. And the sound of the wailing dead in that necropolis was enough to send the mind tottering toward madness. It was detailed in the manuscript that the walkers among the gray world could transport themselves in and out of that place freely and, while there, even manage to bring back objects never meant for the mortal realm.

William paused at that.

Lauren hadn't tried to bring the moss back. She had swallowed it while drowning in whatever gray body of water that had tried to kill her. A question rolled off the precipice of his mind and fell into his stomach.

Can you die in the gray world?

Another question splashed down into his guts.

What happens to your soul if you do?

William read page after page detailing a particular method the women used to enter the gray world. In modern scholarship, these trance-like states were referred to as Diviner's Wells because of the sinking sensation into darkness mediums often described. Though William read over many times to memorize the steps of that process for Lauren to try, it became painfully clear there was no record or indication of the *risk* that one was taking when diving into the well. Nor did it say how the women protected themselves from the occupants of that parallel reality. And just as importantly, how they got themselves out of that meditative trance. The Romani mediums, the manuscript explained, went into the gray world to 'dream walk' or communicate with long-lost family members, loved ones, friends. One particular account described a dream walker bringing back the wedding ring to soothe the broken heart of a childless widower. Surprisingly, not a single Romani account illustrated the gray world as something to fear . . . even though its descriptions terrified William from the perch of his imagination. And the Romani women never detailed spirits attacking the medium.

That was both unique to Lauren and unrecorded by Romani. William wondered if that was something that was made possible by the supernatural magnetism of Black Wells. The exorcist wasn't about to send Lauren into a reality where she could be harmed by a whole army of the dead likely roaming beneath the mundane skin of the city.

And that was where the account ended, with von Junzt leaving the Romani people behind, their experiences recorded.

William rubbed his eyes, allowing the taut line of his concentration to slacken. There was information here, but not much in the way of answers. He had the method of the meditative trance, but because he could not reason it to be safe, he didn't know if he could allow Lauren to engage in its potential danger.

Compared to the gray world, demons were simple. They had known rules upon which an exorcist could rely. Exorcism was often times a chess match. The gray world was a topography. A whole world with undefined rules and undocumented perils. William cursed von Junzt for his lack of thoroughness. He sighed. He wasn't really angry with von Junzt. William was angry at himself.

A better investigator would have come away with something more. Something that could actually stop these manifestations from attacking Lauren whenever they had the strength to do so.

Then, while William inclined his tired head toward the pamphlet on the desk, he saw something that had not been there before.

A cup of coffee.

He picked up the cup and tested it. The liquid was bitter in his mouth, cool on his tongue.

Had Marvin bought him the coffee he'd requested?

How long ago was that?

Then, he heard something. A sentence spoken behind him. The voice, which was not one, but many.

"You will fail, William."

William snapped around, startled.

Nothing.

He swallowed hard.

When was the last time he'd taken communion?

When had he last taken his medication?

"We see," the voices said in unison.

The voices laughed, their sound like ancient thunder.

He snatched up his things and opened the door.

The windows outside, which had sparkled with morning sunlight when he entered the reading room, were darkened with night.

William cursed and hurried down the steps.

"Can you see, William?"

The voices were louder now, thunder becoming the whip-crack of a lightning strike. The shock of which almost sent him tumbling down the stairs.

Through the glass floors he could see down into the lobby. Marvin's circular desk was empty.

So were the lobby chairs.

"Can you hear, William?"

At the bottom of the stairs, William rushed toward Marvin's desk and called out for Lauren. His voice echoed through the cavernous library.

"We have sinned, Father William Daniels. And it has been an eternity since our last confession."

The voices laughed again.

"Marvin!" The exorcist damned the rules of the archive.

"*Will you hear our confession?*"

"Shut the fuck up!"

He had to get to his chalice in the office. It was only a ten-minute drive. He would go there, take communion and his medication, then come back and figure out where—

"*Where to begin . . .*"

William tried to draw his concentration taut again, tried to focus. Bounding across the lobby, he pulled on the door to exit.

"*1989.*"

William froze.

"*I remember,*" said the voices as one. "*My hands around your throat . . . in your son's bedroom.*"

The exorcist's hand, suddenly slathered in sweat, slid away from the brass handle of the door.

"*Yes. You remember.*"

The voice was so clear, so real. Coming from behind him.

He turned.

Standing before Marvin's circular desk, there was a crowd of figures. Men, women, and children of all sorts and colors, each of them dressed in a black suit. Their mouths moved in unison.

"*We remember.*"

"You," said William, an old hatred flashing up in him like a fire.

All of the faces, young and old, smiled needle-tipped smiles.

"*Yes, motherfucker.*" The horde mocked him. "*Us.*"

William's anger sent him running again, but not for the door. He ran toward the crowd, swearing to God that he would kill them all.

The crowd embraced him in a wave, cascading over

him with their many hands, driving the exorcist and his impotent rage to the ground. And the sharp, jagged fingers of the crowd plunged into his mouth, yanking his jaw open. They tore his clothes open, splayed him out, holding him by each limb. William thrashed with all his strength, but they held him fast. He bit down on the fingers as hard as he could. One of the horde cried out, sliding her hand out of his mouth.

Those who did not hold him down parted, so that before the prostrate exorcist stood one, taller and more prominent than the rest.

William knew that face.

It was the face of the man who had murdered his wife and child.

John Terry Brock.

"I will kill you!" William screamed.

"You cannot kill the eternal. Cannot jail that which escaped heaven's chains, exorcist."

The creature in the form of man straddled William, setting his tremendous weight on the exorcist's chest. The pressure drove the wind from William's lungs.

"Shhh," the demon placed a finger to his lips. *"Now, I want you to listen to my confession. I want you to know exactly what it was like in the room when I lifted your first-born by the neck and did this . . ."*

The demon wrapped its fingers around William's throat.

With an impossible strength, he began to squeeze.

William struggled, but it was in vain. And a gray curtain drew in from the sides of his vision. The gray, flat color of the other side. The color of death.

Chapter Fifteen

Lauren

Lauren **had just** finished her second cup of mint tea when she heard the screams. She snapped her eyes over to Marvin, whose posture shot arrow-straight and his head craned upward to peer wide-eyed through the glass ceilings.

Without looking at Lauren, his hands probed behind the desk. "Stay here," he commanded, his voice bell-clear and direct. When he rushed out of the desk, Lauren saw the glimmer of something metallic in his hand.

It was a revolver.

"Wait," shouted Lauren. "What are you doing with that?"

"Stay *there*."

Another bellowing scream shattered itself upon the walls of the cavernous repository.

"Oh, to hell with that." Lauren shoved herself out of the lounge chair and chased after the archivist. By the time she reached the third floor, the man was already at the door of the reading room.

"Mr. Daniels!"

Lauren tried to call out to the exorcist, but the flight had taken it out of her. She bent over, hands on her knees trying to catch her breath.

"Mr. Daniels," Marvin yelled, trying to turn the doorknob. It didn't budge.

"What are you doing with a gun!?"

Marvin ignored the question. "*William*!"

"Why would . . . " Lauren huffed, and sucked in a breath. "Why would he lock the door?"

"These doors don't *have* locks," Marvin said, wrenching all of his weight to try and twist the knob.

"Kick it open!"

Marvin swung his weight back onto his heels, and shot his foot forward. His heel slammed into the brass plate just under the knob. The door stood firm.

William stopped screaming.

Again and again, the archivist kicked at the door, screaming for William to answer.

Marvin swung his foot back again, but just before he kicked forward, the door clicked. Then, it opened only a sliver, slowly creaking on its ancient hinges. Marvin put a hand against the door and lifted the pistol. He pushed.

The door swung wide. William was facing away from them, seated in a chair before a large, red desk.

Marvin swung the office chair around.

William's eyes bulged in his head, their mismatched colors flashing with panic. His skin was a bluish hue and his mouth was open. The exorcist's upper torso convulsed with the spasms of asphyxiation.

"He can't brea—"

Lauren stopped short when she saw his neck. The skin was compressed inward, discolored with the redness of pressure.

"Something's choking him!"

With his empty hand, Marvin contorted his fingers strangely and then, with a small sweeping gesture, made a sign in the air. He spoke a word under his breath.

William's chest heaved. The skin around his neck relaxed and he let out a long, raspy exhalation. Like a taut rope suddenly gone slack, he slid out of the chair and slumped to the ground.

Lauren shoved Marvin out of the way and flipped William over. She pressed two fingers into his neck, checking for a pulse.

Nothing.

"Will!" Lauren called out. Then placed her interlaced hands upon his chest. "Come on, Will!" Just before she began compressions, William sucked in a breath.

William twisted onto his side, pressing his weight into Lauren's knees. His legs and arms shook violently and his voice trembled with desperate, humming inhalations.

"Thank you, Lauren," said Marvin. "Now, if you please . . . "

From behind her, Lauren heard the sound of the revolver's hammer ratchet back.

"Step away."

Lauren gasped. Marvin was pointing the pistol at Will.

"Stop! What—"

"My job is to protect the archive at all costs." He swiveled, aiming the pistol inches from Lauren's forehead. "I would hate to have to shoot you, too."

Lauren said nothing, scooting away from writhing William.

Marvin nodded at her politely. "Thank you." The gun's killing end shifted back to William.

"Say something, Mr. Daniels," said Marvin, his tone cold and heavy as the gun in his hand.

William, his breath almost regained, croaked. "Something happened."

"Of that we are painfully aware, sir. Now, if you would so kindly, tell me a truth."

"Are you fucking insane?" cried Lauren. "Can't you see—"

"Your father—" He hacked again, but found his breath. "Your father's name is Simon Kasdan."

Marvin kept the gun on him. "And another."

"He adopted you. Brought you up to take his place when he retired."

"And a final one, Mr. Daniels."

"You would pull that trigger without hesitation if you caught me in a lie."

Marvin slowly levered the hammer of the revolver forward and set the gun against his thigh.

Lauren let out a breath she hadn't even known she'd been holding. "What the hell happened, Will?"

"I—"

"Mr. Daniels," Marvin cut him off. "I am going to ask you and Lauren to please exit the premises. I am revoking your access to the archive, effective immediately. When you have sorted out whatever it is you have denied telling me about your own situation, then I will consider reinstating your privileges."

"Wait, *why*?" Lauren asked.

William gripped the lip of the desk and rose.

"Because, while Mr. Daniels didn't lie to me, he is certainly hiding something, and whatever that is, it placed the safety of the archive at risk. That is an infraction I cannot and will not tolerate."

"Marvin," William began.

"No, William," said Marvin, an iron authority in his voice.

William nodded, still using the desk to steady himself.

They made their way down into the lobby, Marvin behind them the entire time. No one spoke. Lauren exited first, stepping into the bitter cold night.

William, gripping the brass, vertical handle of the large oak door, turned and looked back to Marvin. "For what it's worth, Marvin, thank you."

"I have been the caretaker of the archive for nearly eight years, Mr. Daniels. My father for the fifty years prior to that. Only once during his tenure was he required to use the sign of banishment. My father never allowed that person to enter the archive again. Not because the sign was required, but because it was a lie that brought forth its use."

"I understand."

"I will inform your patron of the situation." Marvin adjusted his glasses and straightened his tie.

"No need. Trust me, I'll do it."

Marvin's thin lips pressed together tightly, clearly holding back something he wanted to say. "Then your patron will hear of it from the both of us. From me, immediately. Your jacket, coat, and tie will all be sent to your office via courier tomorrow."

William didn't reply.

The door closed.

A tumble of a lock fell into place.

The exorcist looked at the door for a moment, silent.

"Are you okay?" asked Lauren.

"I need to go to my office," he said weakly. "I'll need you to drive."

"Are you sure that's a good idea?"

"Between the two of us, Lauren, it's safer if you're behind the wheel. You're in a more stable state than me."

"*I* am the more stable one?"

William dropped his keys in her hand as he walked past her. "Hurry. I don't know how long I have."

It became very clear, very quickly, that one did not *drive* the Mercury so much as one pointed it in a general direction. The big, lumbering automobile took turns the way a boat glided around a dock. Lauren jumped two curves before she figured that out.

She apologized both times, but William said nothing. He stared out the window, speaking only to give directions to his office. Even though Lauren knew how to get there from her trip yesterday, she simply acknowledged each of his statements.

Just as they pulled up to the darkened building, William said, "I'm going to ask you to be a part of something. Something I haven't shared with anyone, Lauren. It will be strange to you, but I need you to trust that I know what I am doing."

And that was a problem. Lauren *didn't* trust him at the moment. From Sarah to Marvin, the main issue everyone seemed to have with William was his inability to be straightforward about things.

Lauren sighed. "I need you to tell me what's about to happen, Will."

"Once we get inside—"

"Now."

William grit his teeth in frustration. "*Alright*. You're going to come into my office and you're going to make sure I do two things, and that I don't do anything else before I do those two things."

"Those being?"

"I'm going to swallow two pills from a red container in the top drawer of my desk," he said, rubbing his eyes. "Then, I'm going to take communion."

"What medication?"

"Does it matter?"

"I'm a nurse, Will. Of course it matters."

"There is no *time for this*, Lauren. Right now, my brain is on a countdown that, for all I know, is seconds from zero. And just as important, so is yours. If we both have attacks at the same time, I'm probably going to die and so are you."

Lauren froze. The world seemed to elongate, time stretching with it.

William balled his hands into fists. "Those are possibilities, Lauren. And I swear to God, I'm doing everything in my power to make sure they don't happen. Now can you please, just *help* me, so that I can help you?"

There was pain and desperation in his face that Lauren could not only see, but feel, too. It wasn't the same kind of weight she'd been carrying, but she was starting to guess that it wasn't all that different either.

"*William Daniels is a single pin-prick of light amid an irrepressible darkness . . .*" Lauren remembered Sarah's words she'd spoken over dinner the night before.

"*Will shoulders a crushing weight I can't even imagine . . .* " she had said. Lauren saw that oppressive weight on him now. His skin was clammy and damp. Eyes bloodshot. The deathly pallor of dangerous exhaustion masked his face.

"Okay, Will. Let's get you what you need."

Inside, the marble floors glowed eerily from the shafts of gloomy noon-daylight slanted against their slick surface. Lauren tried to examine the glass representation of St. Michael, but the archangel was hidden in shadows. The building was cooler than before, though not quite cold enough to make a vapor of their breath. Their footfalls echoed among the stones. William leaned heavily on the iron railing, taking each step slowly.

William had obviously come back after he'd dropped her off at Sarah's. The mess that her attack had left had been cleaned and the chairs were back inside the waiting room when William snapped on his office light.

"In here," said William, who entered his office proper. Lauren followed him inside.

The inner office was larger than Lauren had expected. There was a desk littered with envelopes and what looked like a photograph that William quickly shuffled into a drawer. He opened another drawer and pulled out a half-empty bottle of whiskey and two glasses. Then he reached down again, producing a slender bindle and a small, silver cup. The cup was ornately shaped with a white cross enameled into the silver. One final time, he reached down and brought out a red cylinder topped with a white cap.

"Medication," he said. "I will take two of them." He said these things out loud but it did not seem like he was saying them for Lauren so much as he was saying them for himself. Looking at the clock, he said. "It is 12:46 A.M. and I am taking two pills."

"Helps you remember?"

William popped the pills into his mouth, poured

himself a drink, and washed them down. "Yeah," he said with the dry rasp brought forth from the heat of the whiskey.

"Really. You shouldn't be taking whatever that is with alco—"

"It's fine. Now, have a drink with me." He poured another drink for him, then a smaller one for her.

He lifted the glass and extended it to Lauren. "It'll help us both for what's next."

Lauren took the glass.

William reached over with his own and clinked them together. "Against the snares of the devil."

"Uh, sure."

He drank deeply.

Lauren swirled the whiskey in the glass.

"Drink," he said. "Doesn't work if you don't."

"Wait. Really?"

William grinned. "No." He unfolded the bindle, revealing two silver cylinders. One Lauren didn't recognize. The other she did.

"Is that a syringe?"

"Yes," he said, rolling up his shirt sleeve.

"You're going to inject yourself with something."

"No," he replied, then he pulled a short section of plastic tubing from the open desk drawer. He wrapped it around his bicep, tied it off. His lighter was in his hand next and, striking the flame to life, he picked up the syringe and held the needle end over the flame.

"You don't have any alcohol wipes?"

"This is easier," he said. "Look, this is all very strange. Believe me, I know. What I also know is that this works. I don't exactly know why. I just know that it does. And I can't trust myself right now with anything sharp. So, I'm going to need you to draw my blood to the full measure of the syringe. Then, you will deposit that blood into the cup here." He tapped the needle against the silver chalice.

A cold realization came into Lauren's mind. "What are you going to do with the blood once it's in the chalice?"

She knew the answer before he said it.

"I'm going to drink it. After I consecrate it, of course."

"Will, do you know that it is dangerous to ingest large amounts of blood?"

"Yes."

"It causes iron poisoning."

"It's almost more dangerous for everyone if I don't do this. Especially me."

"I can't do this. This is self-harm. It goes against . . . "

"Lauren. The clock is ticking. We can discuss your Hippocratic Oath afterward. You will do more harm by not helping than if you do. Please."

Lauren sighed and shook her head. Then she lifted the glass of whiskey to her lips and drank it all in one gulp. She didn't taste the whiskey, only felt the burn. She angrily set the glass on the table and pulled one of the consulting chairs around to the side of the desk. Sitting down, she took the syringe from William.

Lauren quickly found the red dimple in the crook of his elbow. The man's veins were amply plump from the constriction of the tube. With a practiced, professional series of movements, Lauren watched the dark, almost blue blood draw into the syringe via a little glass section cut into the silver body. When it was full, she found a pocket handkerchief on the desk and set it over the injection site. "Hold that here," she said, a reflex.

She drew out the needle and deposited the blood into the silver cup. The blood ejected red and thick, bubbling at the bottom.

William bent his elbow, putting his hand close to his ear. With his other hand he popped the cap of the second cylinder, tapping its open mouth onto the desk.

A little circular wafer with a cross pressed into the cracker flipped onto the desk.

"Thank you," he said. He closed his eyes, and began to whisper.

William made the sign of the cross over the cup with his hand holding the wafer. Then, he placed the wafer on his tongue, lifted the bowl, and drank.

The sound of his swallows were thick, low noises. And when he pulled the chalice from his mouth, his lips were red with lukewarm blood.

Lauren let her weight fall back against the chair, getting a little distance between herself and the man whose pale skin and bright lips gave him the appearance of a vampire.

"So that's it," she said, putting things together in her mind. "That's what keeps those . . . demons in their cells?"

William dabbed his mouth with the handkerchief. "Yes."

"What happened at the library . . . that's what happens if you don't do this?"

"Only the second time it has ever happened. The first time I only heard voices, so I repeated the ritual, and now do it at least once a day. This time . . . this time . . . it tried to kill me."

Lauren blew out a breath. "That's really fucked up."

"If you think that about my strange kind of communion, then you might not be ready for what I'm going to tell you about *your* problem."

"I'm not drinking anyone's blood, Will."

Wiping the corners of his mouth, William let himself chuckle; it was a humorless sound. "No blood," he promised. "But you are going to take a trip."

"Where?"

"First to my place, where I can set out a safe place for you."

"That's what you said about Sarah's."

"I know. I'm sorry."

"Then?"

William's voice grated to gravel. "To the other side. A place Conrad von Junzt and the Romani mediums—women just like you—called the Gray World."

Chapter Sixteen

William

Before anyone was set to attempt an occult ritual or venture into any damn supernatural vista, they were going to eat first. Which is why on their way to his house, William went through the twenty-four-hour drive-thru of the Burger Out. The food was cheap, hot, and by the time they pulled up to his house it had turned the brown paper bag black with grease.

Lauren grabbed the food.

William grabbed her luggage from the trunk.

"Here it is," said William, sliding his key into the slot.

"I honestly half-expected it to be a basement underneath an abandoned church," Lauren said.

"Oh, that's the summer house. This is just a roof to keep the rain off my head." He pushed the door open and flipped on the light. "Ladies first."

Lauren looked around. "The world's foremost exorcist lives in a place that looks like it was decorated by my grandfather." She pointed. "Is that an actual grandfather clock?"

"I like things that are reliable," he said, stepping around her to head back into the kitchen. "Table is back this way. You can set the food down there. Make yourself comfortable."

Lauren didn't follow him into the kitchen, but instead

peered around the parlor just left of the hall. "By reliable, you mean old."

William set her luggage down in the living room, navigating his way between a set of wingback chairs facing the darkened fireplace. "Want anything to drink with your burger?"

"What have you got?" she called across the house. "Wait . . . is that a violin?"

He walked into the parlor. Lauren was standing in front of a large bookshelf, leaning forward to look at the viola set among William's personal collection of books and effects.

"It's a viola," he said. He nodded toward the northern part of the house. "Kitchen is this way. I've got beer, whiskey, coffee, and water."

"A beer would be great," she said, following him toward the small kitchen table.

He grabbed four beers from the fridge and met Lauren at the table.

She was pulling the burgers and fries out of the sopping wet sack, setting them at opposing seats. "So, you play the viola."

He cracked the top on two of the beers. Handed one to her.

"Thanks," she said, taking it.

William drank the first beer quickly, draining the bottle to nothing but air in half-a-dozen hard swallows. The harsh, cold burn greeted him like an old friend. He could see Lauren watching him, and her eyes widened when he set the empty bottle down and opened a second.

"Hard day at the office, huh?"

William sat down, peeling open the white paper matted to the double-meat, double-cheese glory set before him. "My mother never let our family eat before everyone was seated at the table. All these years, and still I can't take a bite until . . . "

"Oh," Lauren sat down and started in on her curly fries.

It took William about ninety seconds to wolf down most of the burger. When the food hit his stomach, he felt the heavy blanket of exhaustion fall over him.

"So, you going to tell me what happened in that reading room?" Lauren asked, the mouth of the bottle set against her bottom lip. She took a swig.

William considered the question, probing a section of chewed-up meat stuck to his teeth. "Sure," he said. "First, how's your head? See anything strange or feel that unsettled sensation?"

"Nope. Normal, I guess. I think this burger might blow up my stomach, but nothing other than that."

"Good," he said, leaning back against his chair. "I got some information that we're going to be able to use, I think. It's risky, but at this point, I feel like it's the best chance we have, considering what happened at Sarah's."

"Okay . . ."

"What happened at the Kasdan Archive was I got sloppy. I allowed myself to lose track of time and went too long without doing what you saw me do in my office. Because of that, the entities inside me got a chance to express their will. Or, at least one of them did."

"It wanted to kill you?"

William thought about that. "I don't know if it wanted to kill me. But, it certainly wanted me to know that we'd met before. It wanted me to be afraid. It wanted me to suffer. Demons feed on suffering. The more I suffer, the stronger it becomes. The more strength it has over its victim, the more it can manifest its will in the natural world. Possession works a lot like a snowball rolling down a hill. The demon is the snow and the victim is the hill; the longer the snow rolls, the more control it gains. The younger the victim, the steeper the slope. But the slope for a child is much shorter. Demons roll quickly, gain power quickly."

"What happens when the snowball runs out of hill?" asked Lauren.

"The ball keeps rolling, looking for another hill. Spends its momentum possessing someone else, only to roll again."

"What about older people?"

"Adults, even teenagers post-puberty, they're taller, but their minds have had a chance to mature, gain wisdom and have a more secure sense of self. Slighter slope, but a taller hill to roll down. A demon gets inside an adult long enough, they can manifest enough will to cause an avalanche."

A thought, clear as a meteor in the night sky, flashed over Lauren's face.

"What?" he asked.

"Nothing. I just—"

"It's okay, go ahead."

"Are you sure that taking these demons into your mind doesn't . . . I mean, are you sure they aren't snowballs rolling down Mount Saint William?"

William shook his head. "No. If I were possessed, you'd be able to tell."

"Like how?"

"Well, for one, I would forsake sunlight. I'd show an extreme aversion to holy objects. Like, say, these delicious carnival style fries." He shoved a few into his mouth, almost comically.

Lauren laughed.

William smiled, liking the sound. "I sure as hell wouldn't be able to take communion."

"That makes sense."

"Right, but I like your thinking. No, I'm not possessed. I'm something else and whatever that is, the demons trapped inside me are very unhappy about it."

"So . . . what happened in the room?"

William took a long swallow of his beer. "One of the demons manifested himself to me, drew me into a dream or some kind of hallucination. And there, it proved that we'd met before, about eleven years ago when the demon had possessed a man named John Terry Brock."

The memories came flooding back to him. He set the second empty bottle down on the table and twisted open the third. And without thinking, he just started. Didn't know why. No one asked. It just . . . happened.

"In 1989, I wasn't an exorcist. I was . . . someone else. Happily married with a child, working as an ancient history professor at a college you've never heard of. Happy," he said again.

"I came home on the night of October 24th to a silent house. And when I went upstairs, into my son's bedroom, John Terry Brock was standing next to his bed. He had just finished strangling my boy to death."

"That's . . . oh my God, William . . . "

William nodded. "We wrestled to the ground. I was screaming. Fought each other. I hit him over and over. And he just took it, with his face mangled John Terry Brock laughed in my face. He was stronger than me," said William, falling back into that wild, harrowing catastrophe. "He shoved me onto the bed, Lauren. Right where my son's body lay . . . lay lifeless. Pinned me down. 'What are you gonna do,' he said. Kept saying it over and over. 'What are *you gonna do?*' Shoved my face into the body. The blood that streaked across my face—still warm." William was there again. Though he stared at Lauren, in his mind, he was looking into the flat, dead eyes of his son. "I could smell the shampoo clinging to his blonde hair. Still damp from the bath."

"Will . . . I'm—I'm so sorry."

Tears welled in William's eyes. He set the beer down, continuing. "My son and I had picked up whittling in this dumb cub scouts knockoff group. I managed to get his whittling knife off his nightstand, next to a half-finished piece of pine he had been working into a lion." He shook his head, doing nothing to wipe the tears falling down his sunken cheeks. "He loved lions. Loved their strength . . . their majesty."

Lauren reached over to place a hand on his. To comfort.

William drew back, the distance more a comfort than the prospect of the touch.

"I whirled on him, slashing him across the face. And when I did, his mouth opened wide. Wider than I had ever seen anyone's mouth open. And he grabbed me by the shoulders with a hideous strength; the demon inside of John Terry Brock had enough momentum inside of that man to pour itself into me. I had no clue, of course, but I remember the world closing like an iris around me. And I heard voices, voices that spoke as one. I battled against it, Lauren. With everything I had. My anger and my sorrow. Fought with each inch of love for my child. The demon only taunted me, lied to me."

William gritted his teeth.

"Cheated me out of everything."

"How did you get rid of it?"

"I didn't. I woke up inside of a hospital. The police told me they'd found me at the scene unconscious. And that both my wife and son did not survive the home invasion." William shook his head, his anger boiling his brow sweaty. "*Home invasion*," he repeated the cruel irony. "The police found Brock at his home a couple days later. He'd hanged himself with an electrical cord in the shower. A weeks passed, and that's when I started hearing the voices. Voices in my head. Many voices speaking as one. I checked myself into a psych ward and after a few months of intense, failed psychotherapy I was visited by a Catholic priest—Father Julio Jorge Rodriguez. The first exorcism I was a part of was my own. Father Julio saved my mind. Took me in. Then he saved my life by taking me to a Benedictine monastery and trained me to become an exorcist."

Lauren just stared at him, an overwhelming sense of pity on her tired, tear-soaked face. "What were their names?"

William opened his mouth to speak, but the words caught in his throat. He smiled an embarrassed, trembling smile, a smile only possible when the scars of grief are reopened. He swallowed hard. "Candice, she was my wife. My s-son's name was Solomon. Solomon Carter Williams. Solomon from Candice's father."

"Carter from you, I'm guessing?" she asked.

"Yeah."

Lauren nodded. "William Carter Daniels," she said, a smile crossing her lips. "Now you've captured the thing that killed them."

William struggled, but spoke through aching, clamped teeth. "I have," he said. "And I am going to find a way to destroy it. Which is quite the trick, considering they are probably immortal. But if I can't, Lauren. I'm going to shove it down into a pit so deep, and so dark, it'll make Hell look like Heaven. I'll paint a red prison around it for the rest of my life."

"Does Sarah know . . . about your family?"

William shook his head.

"Doctor Irving?"

"No. No one does. Except, now, you."

Lauren exhaled heavily. After a moment of searching her own mind, she said, "Why tell me?"

William laughed his unhappy laugh. "I don't know. I think sometimes people just get tired of holding onto their own stories. Their own pain. I just lasted longer than most. Lucky you, that you were in my company the moment the dam broke."

Lauren reached over again, insistent, and placed a soft hand over his.

William let it happen this time.

"I'm glad I was, Will. Sarah was right about you."

"Right about what?"

"She said that you shoulder a weight heavier than she can imagine. And now, I know just how right she was."

William felt the warmth of Lauren's hand on his own. The smoothness of kindness sliding over his skin reminded him of just how long it had been since he'd touched another human being in a comforting way. "To answer your question: the viola isn't mine. It was my wife's," he said slowly. "I don't play. She did."

Lauren smiled. "I am sure she was wonderful."

William squeezed her thumb, then slid his hand back to the beer. "I don't think I'm in a place to try the thing I found at the archive, Lauren. My mental faculties are compromised. And what we're going to attempt will require the very best of our concentration and will. Do you feel comfortable trying to get some sleep, give it a go in the morning?"

Worry masked Lauren's face, but she pressed her lips together resolutely, saying, "I think you're right. I feel safe with you. I trust you."

William nodded, and they sat there a little while longer in silence. He showed Lauren to the guest room. Brought her things and told her goodnight even though it was only 5:30 P.M. He fell asleep in his own bed. The cold, empty sheets reminding him of everything he had lost.

Chapter Seventeen

Lauren

It was still dark outside when Lauren woke from her dreamless sleep. The smell of bacon roused her from her bed, the sizzling sound led her from the sparse guest room. In the kitchen, she found William Daniels standing over a cast-iron skillet.

"Morning," he said.

"Good morning." Lauren tried to rub the grogginess from her eyes.

"Coffee is next to the fridge. Cups are just above it." He flipped the bacon.

"Thanks."

Lauren poured herself a cup and sat at the table. She reached over and started picking up the paper burger wrappers, feeling bad that she hadn't helped clean up the night before.

"Don't worry about that," said William.

"It's no problem. Really."

There was a strange tension in his voice and Lauren took note that William was staring at the cooking meat far more than necessary. "Is everything okay?"

"I'm sorry about yesterday," he said. "I shouldn't have unloaded all of that on you. With all the things going on in your life, I'm sure it wasn't very helpful to have me drop everything on you like that. I'm supposed

138

to be helping you, not hitting you with my emotional baggage."

"It didn't bother me at all," she said, dropping the wads of greasy paper into the brown paper sacks they'd originally come in. "It's kind of . . . relieving to know that other people have had experiences that I can relate to."

"You'll find a lot of that here in Black Wells if you go looking for it. I know almost a dozen people who live the kind of lifestyle Sarah and I live. We all try to be available to each other if we run into something that falls outside of our professional sphere. Sarah is helpful when magic is involved. One of my best friends is sort of a historian of the supernatural. Hell, my mechanic is a cryptid hunter."

Lauren tossed the paper sack into the garbage bin. "And you're the guy who knows about demons."

William half-saluted her with the spatula in his hand. "That's me. But, there are more things in heaven and earth than are dreamt of."

"With all those people doing those kinds of things, I'm guessing Marvin is a pretty important player."

William nodded. "Marvin is the greatest source of supernatural reference in Black Wells, maybe the world. His father Simon was the original caretaker of the Kasdan Archive. They share a remarkable story that's tied closely to Black Wells's history."

"Losing that resource has to be a big blow to your work," said Lauren, going back to her coffee.

"Yeah," William said in the form of a long, mournful sigh. "But them's the breaks. Speaking of my work, anything from the other side this morning?"

Lauren dared to look around William's house. She didn't see any drowned corpses; didn't see or smell anything; and the only tension in the room was between her and the exorcist making her breakfast. "Nothing," she said.

"Well, that's going to change after breakfast."

They ate together, mostly in silence. William only ate a few strips of bacon, while Lauren coupled hers with three over-easy eggs and another mug of coffee. When William was done eating, he slid his plate away and produced his pipe. After he took a few puffs from the lighted bowl, he said, "Today is going to be difficult, Lauren. I'm going to ask a lot from you. It'll take all of your courage and your will. A lot of trust. If you want to back out, now is the time to do it."

"There isn't any backing out of this, Will."

He nodded, the smoke billowing over his lips. "Right. But for what it's worth, I needed that to come from you."

"I'm willing to do whatever it takes to get my life back," she said, running her thumb through the condensation dewed on her glass.

"That's the right attitude. You have the advantage of already having witnessed the kind of things you'll see once you start your trance—"

"Trance?"

"You'll go into a deep, meditative state where we're going to try and open all of your senses to the other side. From what I have read, it'll be a version of our reality. It will appear to you as a gray, desolate place that mirrors our own geography. While you are there, I'm going to ask you to look for the three women who have been visiting you."

Lauren nervously licked her lips. "I thought the goal was getting away from them?"

"There is no running from these spirits that have latched onto you. They've found your . . . let's call it a wavelength, and they use it like a beacon. When they interact with you, they can touch the physical world again. Their voices can be heard. And I think they're doing that because they have something important to say."

"So now I'm a radio transmitter for the dead. Great."

William shook his head. "Not a radio, Lauren. You're a livewire. And a very powerful one, from what I've gathered.

Most mediums have one, maybe two, senses that can detect these things. They can see or hear things from the other side, but very, very few can bring something else over from the other side like you did. It's exceedingly rare."

"Yippee." Lauren stabbed the last sliver of bacon on her plate dismissively.

"It could be worse," he said.

"Yeah?" Lauren gave him the same unimpressed look as before. "How?"

"You could have a parade of demons trying to actively drive you insane." He smiled.

The tension between them finally relaxed and Lauren asked, "When do we get started?"

"That depends."

"On what?"

"On if you're done with breakfast."

Lauren picked up the last piece of bacon on her plate, considered it, and took the absolute smallest bite possible.

William laughed.

Lauren laughed, too, almost spitting out the bacon.

"You're going to do great," he said.

Ten minutes later, the kitchen tidied, Lauren sat on a circular rug cross-legged in the middle of William's living room. He walked around her several times, pouring salt onto the rug in concentric rings. The lines of exhaustion that had masked his face earlier were now replaced with hard lines of concentration. The salt fell to the floor like a crystalline waterfall out of a blue box, and the exorcist had lit several candles and a stick of musty incense. Lauren swallowed hard, feeling her heart quicken. All that had seemed like theory and suggestion now became tangible to her.

This was going to happen.

"So, is this a 'light as a feather, stiff as a board' kind of thing?" said Lauren.

William continued pouring the salt until he finished

the third, outermost ring. His voice was all business as he headed toward the kitchen. "Afraid not. I'm going to walk you through a series of relaxation exercises, then I'll ask you to focus on something. If we do this right, the color of the world will wash out. That's when you'll be in the gray world."

"Focus on what?"

He returned carrying a white bowl filled to the brim with water. "We'll get there. One step at a time," he said, setting the bowl down. Then he pulled one of the leather chairs away from the fireplace to sit directly in front of her.

"Just in case I get thirsty?" She smiled.

"It's a lifeline. Water, like salt, is a pure substance. If you get in too deep, or can't find your way out, the water will bring you back."

Lauren nodded, chewing on her lip. "I'm scared."

"I know." He reached into the pocket of his blue cardigan and produced his pipe. He lit it and sat down in the chair. The room was dark, save for the candle flame waving across the exorcist's mismatched eyes and throbbing fire in the bowl of his pipe. "Are you ready?" he asked, the sweet vanilla-smelling smoke wreathing the shadow of his brow.

Lauren wiped her head clear of a few droplets of sweat, her hand cool against her skin. She nodded at him.

"Close your eyes."

Lauren followed his instruction.

"I want you to breathe in deeply. In through the nose. Out through your mouth. Slowly."

Lauren focused on her breathing.

"You are no longer here, Lauren. You are in an empty room. The room is dark, except for a bright light overhead. The light is warm. Comforting. You feel safe here. Do you see it?"

Lauren concentrated, picturing the room inside her mind. The light was a white pool at her feet. The walls came next, sliding up out of the floor, when they reached a great height, the walls curved into a ceiling. "Yes," she said.

"What color are the walls?"

"They're changing color, but . . . green, now."

"The wall in front of you, describe it to me."

Lauren wrinkled her brow, concentrating. In her mind she only saw the blank green surf—

A door appeared. A red door with a silver knob.

"There's a door."

"What kind of door?"

Lauren shook her head, frustrated, but focused on the door. It took a more detailed shape, like the front door of a house. And not just any house.

A house from rural Illinois that had been torn down over fifteen years ago.

Her house.

"It's the front door from the house where I grew up."

"That's good," he said. "I want you to hold on to that good feeling. This is your door, Lauren. And nothing can come through that door, nothing you don't give express permission to. Now, look back at the green walls."

The walls were no longer green, but replaced with cream and scarlet wallpaper. Their color stood like indelible pillars holding up the ceiling. Lauren gasped, suddenly overwhelmed with memory. "My mother's wallpaper," she said. The living room where she had spent hour upon hour playing as a child. The little secretary desk in the corner was the place where she remembered crisp, autumn mornings, her pencil scratching away at her school work. The family's yellow sofa. Her grandmother's coffee table, on which laid her father's 'to-be-read' stack of paperback novels, were there. All of it.

She ran her hand along the sofa, feeling the fabric and the buttons tufting it. So clear. So real.

"It's the house. *My* house."

"Every person's life is a house," William whispered

from some far off place. "The safe architecture where we store our memories; those we remember, and those we think we've forgotten. But the mind never truly loses those things. It keeps them tucked away until they are needed. All our dreams, our fears, hopes; our ghosts. This is your home, Lauren. Your mental fortress. Nothing can interlope here, except that which you allow. "

There was a sound. The sound of footsteps coming from the kitchen. A shadow passed in the doorway and Lauren swore that she could hear a woman humming a happy tune.

Lauren's lips parted. "That song . . . "

"Lauren." William's voice was calm, but stern. "Focus on the door."

"But . . . " The memory the song wrought was powerful. Rich. Coming to life. "My mom used to—"

From out of the kitchen she stepped. A woman, wearing jeans and a man's dress shirt, rolled up at the sleeves. A woman who had died five years ago simply walked back into life again.

"Mom," said Lauren.

The woman turned and looked in Lauren's direction, tilting her head, confused.

"Lauren. I need you to focus on the door," William said.

"But she's right there . . . she's looking at me."

"The door, Lauren." When he said her name again, her mother faded, shimmering out of reality like a mirage.

Tears formed in Lauren's eyes, forced to let go all over again. But she took a deep breath and focused.

"She's gone," said Lauren, hating the way it sounded.

"I want you to walk toward the door, Lauren. I want you to open it and, *before* you go through, tell me what you see."

The carpet was plush on her bare feet and each step made the living room more real to her. The door handle was smooth, cold.

Lauren opened the door.

A blast of icy wind slashed through the initial gap, blowing the door back so abruptly that it nearly knocked Lauren to the floor. A cloud of gray snow swirled in on the blistering wind, so oppressive that she crossed her arms to protect her eyes from the harsh gale. The cold pierced her skin, through bone, down into her soul. It was a painful cold. An emotional cold.

And she did not know how she knew, but it was clear to her that this was a storm not made from any weather system, but a blizzard of suffering and loneliness. The place untouched by the sunlight of paradise and the fires of obliteration. A place so far from both that there was little light. No heat.

It was a cold, cold landscape.

A gray world.

On the wind came the unmistakable sound of the dying. Voices crying together like a thousand cello strings drawn slowly. Wailing together. Almost a song. One could not refuse its melody and to hear it was to sorrow.

Lauren scanned a harrowing horizon.

It was a cratered landscape. A barren waste populated with the gray bones of a gray people howling in unison their gray song. Great towers rose in the distance forged from the pale skin of millions. Maybe more. Beyond them was a mountain; a colorless representation of Black Wells' Astolats. Over that towering, bulk was an eclipse. A cold, black star.

"Lauren." William's voice came from somewhere beyond the gray. "Hear my voice. I want you to remember the faces of the women you saw. Focus on th—"

A shock of gunmetal lightning flashed from a gray cloud rack, so bright that it blinded her. Thunder growled, cascading through the gray streets, all the way to the mountain.

The symphony of the dead receded, leaving only the

distant sound of a few still crying out. Lauren knew those voices, and had heard them for months.

"I hear them," she said.

"Good. Now, follow their sound," replied William.

"You want me to go . . . go outside?"

"Yes."

Lauren stepped over the threshold of her childhood home onto the gray grasses running along an empty street. The moment her foot touched the ground, the gray world populated with the streaming masses of a wandering, gray people wearing the afflictions that had taken life's color. Ashen gunshot wounds gaped in the bodies of the murdered, oozing with soot-shaded blood. She saw in others, gray eyes clouded over with the rheumy fog of what Lauren instinctively knew to be the malignant touch of cancer.

Lauren pressed forward, listening to the trio of voices. Mothers with wide, howling mouths soundlessly cried out toward corpse-filled mounds of small, gray bodies. The cold wind swept across those lifeless faces, briefly straightening their infant curls. Over those desolated moors of lost children, men and women roamed zombie-like. In their staggered meandering they searched aimlessly. What they were looking for Lauren did not know.

Along the gray streets were bruised women shackled in colorless dresses and bloody-knuckled men, whiskey bottles clutched in their shackled hands. The derelict elderly lay in tattered gray hospital gowns, clawing along the ground. All of them too weak to stand. Too weak to cry out.

Over that writhing mass a group of children stood motionless. Only staring. Their wide, desperate eyes screaming to move with the reckless energy death had robbed from them. Overcome, Lauren wept at the witnessing of a landscape completely separated from life or the prospect of a life hereafter. She wept in the knowledge that there was no love here, only fear. No joy, only sadness.

Nothing but the sheer, gray terror of permanent abandonment.

Lauren, arms crossed over her chest in a self-protecting embrace, stepped among these people with an overwhelming sense of pity. She did not fear the gray people as she had the three women who had assaulted her. Instead of fear, she felt an irrepressible desire to help them. That desire chained itself around her heart, and she recognized immediately that the rings of that chain would never loosen, never shatter. To see such a sight changed the seer.

The gray streets wound around flesh-stitched monuments, sloping down into a yawning, slate culvert. A stream trickled out of the aperture, its monochrome surface rippling darkly with the sonic desperation of the women's voices. Chiseled crudely into the arch of the culvert were the words: *Arbeit Macht Frei*. She did not know what it meant, but reading it coiled a thread of ice around her spine.

Lauren avoided the gray waters streaming from the darkness as long as she could, but following the women's cries meant going deeper into the culvert's slope, where the little stream swelled river thick. At first sight, she thought the liquid was water. But when she dipped into its depths it proved cold and viscous, clinging to her. A foul smell rose from it, assaulting her nose. The rancid odor of spoiled eggs and old milk turned her stomach over and she gagged.

Then, from somewhere close, how close she did not know because of the ricocheting acoustics of the tunnel, Lauren heard the water-chopping slap of a panicked swimmer. Over that, there came a fresh volley of screams.

"Elder Marshal," a woman cried out.

"Please . . . stop!" another.

They were the first recognizable words that had come from the gray waste.

"Please!"

Just around the curve of one of the coved concrete tunnels, Lauren came upon a chamber cut into the stone.

There, standing waist deep, was a tall figure. His arms plunged deep into the fluid, weight leaning forward. The gray liquid capping white around him, as he held someone face-down in the depths. The arms of the assailed wildly splashed and clawed, fighting the assaulter. Two women stood on a raised platform, shackled to the wall. They writhed with the unmistakable pallor of hypothermia, starved to skeletal aspect. The sunken basket of their rib cages swelled, the skin stretched taut as wet cotton fabric against the braille of their sternums. Emaciated limbs, cuffed at the wrist and ankles against the cracked concrete of the wall, splayed them wide as spiders set upon a web.

The assaulter, calm and strong, held the woman under the liquid, shushing her gently until her arms ceased to thrash. The surface of the fluid bubbled around the woman's head and after a final, desperate spasm, the violence of her struggle ceased.

The assaulter approached one of the shackled women. When he turned, Lauren saw that the man was wearing a mask. A flat ceramic piece whose only features were slits for eyeholes.

"Stop," the woman near the man cried out. "Please, Marshal. Please. I—"

"Amanda, my dear Amanda," his tone like that of a lover. "Hush, now. You are only feeling the fear of the sacrifice. You cannot yet see what is beyond the pale."

"Marshal, I don't want—"

The man identified as Marshal caressed her cheek. "Will you now, at the precipice of your greatest act of faith, become an apostate? You, who have feasted at the benefit of our Master's benevolent table?"

148

"But I didn't know—"

"You did," his voice kind. Gentle. "You did." The man's head twisted to attention. "There. Do you feel it, Amanda? Can you sense the advent of the great work taking place inside of our dear Sheila?"

From the depths, the liquid around the head of the drowned woman began not to bubble, but to boil. And with the patience of a crocodile ascending to break the placid surface, the floating corpse of the drowned women began to rise. Her hair like black, wet silk hung heavy from the crown of her skull, breaching the water. Then came the eyes, bulbous, penetrating, and black. The dead rose from the water and stood, alive again. Naked, lean as an insect, and unashamed.

"Shelia?" asked the woman on the far side of Elder Marshal and Amanda.

"No," said Marshal. "Not our Sheila. Someone greater."

The once drowned, now reanimated woman stood to her full height, turned, and slowly walked away from Elder Marshal and his captives, back to the culvert entrance.

The woman did not seem to bob in the water with steps, but rather seemed to float.

Float directly toward Lauren.

Lauren froze, looking into the eyes of the pale woman drifting toward her. Those eyes that wore no shade of the gray world, but black. Black and slick like the carapace of a cockroach. To look into those eyes was to fall into an abyssal pit from which there would surely be no return.

Whatever the woman was, she certainly wasn't the person she had been before. She drifted past Lauren, floating by so closely that the gentle wake she cut through the liquid splashed against Lauren's arm.

Where was she going?

Marshal had unshackled Amanda and was roughly pulling her down the slope into the gray pool. And while the third woman screamed for Marshal to stop, the man took a firm grip of Amanda's hair and plunged her face-down into the water.

Turning back, Lauren watched Sheila drift into the gray, until she turned and stepped out of sight.

Something deep inside of Lauren awoke. A ferocity unknown to her in her life before the gray world. Something pure and hot.

What she felt was rage.

Rage at the suffering. The violation.

Lauren screamed and sloshed through the waters toward Marshal. The man did not react, but only smiled and held his victim beneath the water.

"Lauren," a voice cried out from very, very far away.

Lauren ignored it. And with all her strength, she leapt at the masked man killing Amanda.

Her outstretched hands, bent into claws, passed through Marshal. And all her momentum carried her forward, then down. Down into the foul, greasy liquid.

A cold impact slapped Lauren across the face.

Her eyes flew open and the sound that suddenly filled her ears was the sound of her own screams.

The culvert, the gray world were gone. All of it replaced by the concerned face of William Daniels.

Lauren fell over, her fingers digging into the salt ring William had placed around her. She sucked in a wild breath and sobbed. Between gasping breaths she tried to speak.

William threw his arms around her, holding her close. "It's okay. You're here. You're safe."

"He," Lauren said, trembling. "He murdered them."

William pulled Lauren upright. "Who?"

Lauren's face twisted angry. "Marshal," she said. Looking over William's left shoulder, Lauren saw the naked bodies of the three women, facing the wall. Their dark hair dripping. Their bloated corpses slowly turned to look at her.

She was no longer afraid. She looked at the women, unflinching, staring deep into the deep, cold wells of their dead eyes.

"They're here," she said.

"Don't be afraid," he said.

"I'm not," she replied confidently. "They don't want me to be afraid. They want revenge. Revenge for what Marshal did to them." Lauren leveled her eyes hard on William, her voice cold as the wind blowing through the gray world. "And I know where to find him."

Chapter Eighteen

William

From the moment William splashed the bucket of water against Lauren's face, one thing was clear— the woman who had gone into the trance and ventured into the gray world was not the same woman who stood before him now. Lauren Saunders had gone in one thing and returned as something else.

"And I know where to find him." The words didn't sound like a revelation. They were a command.

This was a dangerous time for her. William had experienced this moment many times over during his tenure in Black Wells. The moment when the city itself drew someone into the depths of the shadows always roiling beneath its seemingly mundane surface. It was a delta in the stream of a person's life, choices fanning out before them. William's own moment had been with John Terry Brock and his subsequent exorcism. He had chosen to become an exorcist, facing down the hordes of demonic violators and serve as the lance of St. Michael the archangel that cast out every serpent coiling itself around the souls of the oppressed.

What Lauren would become, William did not know. That future was too complicated for him to see. But what was clear was the rage in the deep pools of blue gazing over his shoulder. He knew that same rage and though his experience taught him it often led down a difficult path, a dangerous, consuming path—it would ultimately be up to Lauren to decide.

"What do you want to do?" William asked.

Lauren didn't hesitate. "It isn't about me. It's about them—what they want. What they demand."

"And what do they want?"

Lauren's ears perked up for a moment, as though she heard some voice William could not. Then, her eyes pierced him. "Vengeance."

"You realize," William said carefully, "that this isn't something the police can help with. If we decide to . . . give them what they want, it will be on you and I to see it through to the end."

Lauren licked her lips, considering the exorcist's words.

He waited.

"What I saw," she said, then took a deep breath. "It was one of the worst—I have to do something. For them."

William nodded. Lauren made her choice and as her helper . . . perhaps even her friend, all he could do was help guide her through what would be a spiral of changes about to happen in her life.

"I understand." Those words could not have been more true. More sincere. "Now," he said, taking the woman by the hand, "tell me everything you saw."

Lauren did just that.

"A faceless mask . . ." Though he knew of many strange cults that resided within the twisting labyrinth of Black Wells's past and present, he had never heard of any particular group using that kind of mask. The ritual was a familiar one—an inversion of the baptismal right within the Christian tradition, but beyond that, he could not ken much. A hot ball of lead dropped into his stomach when Lauren told him of Sheila's black eyes. Was someone using this ritual to send malevolent spirits—or, worse, *demons*—

into reanimated corpses? It made sense. That would allow
a demonic force to bypass a person's will. That meant a
demon wouldn't be *inside* a person . . . but would *become*
that person, able to walk freely in the waking world. It was
a thought that sent his mind back all those years ago during
his struggle with John Terry Brock.

He shoved that thought away.

"Can you find your way back to that culvert?" William
asked her, after she finished.

"Yes."

"We don't know what's there. Or how many cultists
might be residing within. We'll need help."

"Sarah?" asked Lauren.

He shook his head. "No, we don't need a private
detective, and she wouldn't take my call right now anyway.
No, what we need is a tiger."

"Bishop Auto," Karl's low basso voice chimed over the
phone.

"It's me," said William.

"Hopefully, you're calling me from the bank."

"No. Got a scent."

There was a long pause.

"Shop closes at five. Family dinner at six." Karl's voice
dropped lower, darker. "Your office?"

"Yep."

"I'll be there."

The line clicked off.

William Daniels was tamping the ash out of his pipe bowl,
watching Lauren stare out the window of his office when
he heard the eight-cylinder growl of Karl's truck pull up
outside.

"There's our tiger," said William.

Lauren, her arms crossed over her chest. The evening's dying light slanted off her eyes, sparking their blueness like an ocean catching the falling sun.

William tucked his pipe into his pocket. "You're sure—"

"I am."

William nodded. "I understand. That's the last time I'll ask. For what it's worth, it's the last time you'll get the choice. There's no going back after this."

Lauren lowered her head, considering. "For what it's worth, William, there was no going back for me after the nightclub. Just like there was no going back for you the moment you met John Terry Brock. These women deserve their revenge. I want them to have it. Want it more than I've wanted anything."

"I can see that."

"There's something I want to do for me if—if I don't . . . " The fear of potential outcomes masked her face.

"Name it."

"My dad is still alive. If something happens to me, make sure he knows what happened. And that he never comes to Black Wells."

A heavy knock came from the office door.

William got up to answer.

"Promise me," said Lauren.

He stopped in mid-step and nodded, sealing what could likely be their final compact. Then, he stepped into the reception office and opened the door. In the frame stood the wide, bulky figure of Karl Bishop. The big man watched the silver coin flip in the air.

"Come on in," said William.

The coin slapped into Karl's hand. He considered it for a moment, then stepped inside.

"Hope you brought a flashlight," said William, leading the way.

"What's the scent?" Karl was all business.

"Lauren," said William, as they entered his office.

"Meet Karl Bishop—father, husband, damn good mechanic. And, he's the best hunter I've ever met."

"Hi," said Lauren, with a timid wave. "Like, deer hunter?"

"Sure," said Karl, walking over to shake her hand. "Deer, elk."

"Among other things," he said.

"I've known Karl for several years, he's the hammer in case we run into a nail that needs driving, if you catch my meaning."

"Nice to meet you," he said. A big, predatory grin filled his face. "She the medium?" he asked William without looking away from her.

"Yep," William responded.

"Ghost hunt?"

"Cult. Down in the sewers. Guy named Marshal is their elder priest or whatever."

"The sex kind or the violent kind?"

"The kind that does human sacrifices."

Karl let a little hum escape his throat, like he'd just tasted a flavorful wine. "We cannot abide that—can we, Miss Lauren?"

"No," she said, cold as steel. "No we cannot."

"Well then, boys and girl," said Karl. "Let's get to fucking work."

Chapter Nineteen

Lauren

K arl **Bishop drove** a long, black van, the kind typically used for mail delivery. Painted over its sliding door was a portrait of an old, wizened man wrapped in a blue robe with a sword in one hand and a staff in the other. The man in blue was looking back at a knight of some kind, holding a wounded friend in his arms who wore a shining ring chained to his neck.

Karl slid the heavy door open so Lauren could step inside.

"Ladies first."

Inside, there was a single pull-out seat attached to a steel workbench, above which rested an arsenal of guns, bladed weaponry, and cages filled with little, red boxes. Reaching down to pull out the seat from the bench, Lauren noticed a sterling, speaker-shaped drain at the center of the floor, the slick floor rimmed in red.

She pushed away the thoughts of what might have caused it.

William and Karl slid into the captain seats in the front of the van. Karl cranked the engine to life. A monster roared beneath the hood. The headlights blasted forth, cutting white shafts of light into the night.

"Okay, Lauren," said William. "I need you to focus and remember how you got to the culvert."

Lauren focused and receded into her memory, seeing clearly the abhorrent horrors that led to the culvert. It was difficult at first. Nursing school had drilled an ability to remember minute details, but remembering the path was a different skill. And after thirty minutes of driving, filled with turning around and switching back through certain streets, Lauren let out a sigh of frustration.

It was clear that her memory wasn't sufficient for this.

She wouldn't be able to remember the path clearly enough. And so casting out her fear, Lauren took in a deep breath, concentrating. There, inside the childhood home of her mind, she stepped back toward the doorway that led to the gray world. The towering spires of flesh and the moans of the abandoned souls of that place assaulted her. The drone of the van's engine died away, and Lauren listened. Listened for the terrified pleading of the three women.

"Left," she said, her eyes still closed. The van's momentum suddenly shifted, rocking on its shocks to make the turn.

"Lauren . . . . are you—"

The gray world flickered in her mind. The voices fading.

"Quiet," said Lauren. "I'm focusing."

"It isn't safe without the salt rings," he pleaded. "The barrier protects—"

"She said shut up, Padre," said Karl.

Lauren clenched her teeth. Clenched her fists. Focusing not on the gray world or what she saw or what she heard. She focused on the rage. The seething, cold anger that had, from the beginning, roiled out of the three, drowned ghosts.

Sweat dripped down her forehead, down her temples. Lauren threw herself into the depths of her concentration, fueling it with the pain and suffering she'd experienced since moving to Black Wells and all the things that had brought her here.

"Right," she said.

The van squealed.

"Down the embankment."

The gargantuan weight of the van tilted forward, almost pitching Lauren out of her seat.

"Umm, Karl?" Worry filled William's voice. "This isn't a road. You're going to—"

"Have some faith."

Lauren's eyes snapped open. "Here."

The van slowed, then rocked on its shocks to a complete stop. The area around the culvert was filled with non-descript buildings Lauren guessed were a part of the industrial district of Black Wells. The lights of the van illuminated the gaping mouth of the culvert where steam billowed into the cold night from a lattice of steel.

"That's it," she said. "That's the entrance."

"You're sure?" asked Karl.

Lauren pointed at the white spray-painted words crudely written at the arch of the stone, reading, *Arbeit Macht Frei*.

"Yes," she said.

"Arbeit macht frei," said William, the words cold on his lips.

"Gotta be fucking kidding me," Karl said, venom in his words.

"What does it mean?" Lauren asked.

Karl shook his head. "Fucking nazis is what it means."

"I don't understand."

"Work sets one free," said William. "The words written above the entrance of the Auschwitz concentration camp during World War II. Where the Nazis murdered countless innocent people."

"Fucking nazis," Karl said again, even meaner this time.

"The van obviously won't make it past that grate, I'm not even sure *we* can fit through those gaps," said William.

"Not the van, no," said Karl. "But getting us through is a problem that my blowtorch can solve."

Karl worked like a man possessed, wielding the blowtorch with a veteran hand.

"He's good," said Lauren

"Born for it," William replied.

Karl waved them over to help and eventually there was a gap large enough for the three of them to pass through. Lauren and William grabbed large flashlights from the van, while Karl armed himself with a shotgun and a large pistol he slid into a sleeve on the leg of the harness on his waist. He racked a shell into the chamber of the shotgun and said, "Stay behind me. If things go O.K. Corral, drop to your bellies. I don't want you caught in my firing line. Here." He handed a pair of heavy vests to the both of them.

Lauren struggled to put the vest on, but Karl helped her with the straps so that it fit tightly against her chest.

"Shouldn't we have guns, too?" asked William, struggling with his own vest.

Karl sniffed a laugh. "Get a lot of weapons training at the monastery—did you, Padre?"

"No, but—"

"Not happening. You with a gun makes you a danger to yourself and to Lauren. I'm enough gun for whatever is waiting for us at the end of that tunnel."

Lauren's stomach churned and the invisible weight she now associated with the ghostly attacks started to come over her. "I can feel them," she said.

"The women," said William.

"Yes."

"Keep fighting them back, Lauren. Don't let them hurt you now. Not when we're so close."

Lauren shook her head. "They don't want me," she said. "They want whatever is inside that tunnel."

Karl clicked on his flashlight, the beam illuminating a wide, carnivorous grin. "Tell them to get in line."

The three of them walked toward the concrete maw yawning open before them, a curl of moon cut through the clouds in the sky above. They plunged into the dark tunnel, their feet splashing down in ankle-deep water.

The tunnel sloped gently at first, growing steeper the further they traversed. They rounded a coved angle, the lights of the van vanishing behind them. Without those headlights the group had only their flashlights to rely on, the beams of which reached only so far. Karl advised all of them to angle their light toward the walls, while he kept his own close to his feet. Lauren shuffled forward, careful to keep the soles of her feet on the ground. She flashed her light along the left side of the tunnel which revealed long, jagged stress fractures in the wall where green veins of moss clung, dripping. An acrid smell, one that Lauren knew all too well, roiled up from the bowels of wherever the tunnel terminated. The sound of their feet sloshing in the water echoed off the curved concrete.

Though Lauren had been here before, at least in the gray world's version of this place, the darkness and the dripping stone shaped it almost unrecognizable. The anger that had made her nerves strong as steel was drifting from her mind, replaced with uncertainty. With fear. Her stomach cramped, the supernatural tension of the three women was heavily on her now. She tried to massage it away with her free hand, even bending at the waist to alleviate the pressure. Neither helped.

A beam flashed over Lauren, blinding her.

"You okay?" asked William.

Lauren squinted against the light, putting up a hand to protect her eyes. "I can feel them," she said, feeling her lips tremble at the words. "I didn't realize it until now, but they've been pulling me. Trying to get me here."

"Where?" asked William.

Karl's flashlight glanced against a wall. Glinting there,

rusted and wet, where a pair of iron shackles bolted into the stone. She pointed. "There. Where it happened."

"Oh, what the fuck," said Karl.

"Christ in heaven." The words were a curse on the exorcist's lips.

The churning, hot pain inside of Lauren's stomach swelled like a balloon. Her limbs locked painfully at the edge of their joints.

Lauren began to scream with not one voice, but three.

Three voices screaming one word.

Lauren lost herself in that sound.

Chapter Twenty

William

William saw it happen. Saw the oppression take Lauren, as if her whole body had been placed into a vice grip, and squeeze the sound right out of her.

It wasn't Lauren's voice that said, "Elllllllder!"

"The fuck is going on!" Karl swung around at the wailing.

"I don't know," William shouted over the sound. He looked back to Lauren and saw . . .

Christ and all His saints preserve, the words flowing into his mind, the terror of the sight sent his beleaguered apostasy screaming back into the fearful trembling of belief. He made the sign of the cross, a reflex at the sight of Lauren's face.

No, not Lauren. The bloated, rheumy-eyed whiteness of the drowned, eyes that boiled with an inconsolable rage.

Lauren dropped her flashlight and rushed into the darkness. The light died the moment it hit the water.

"Lauren!" William screamed.

The sound of hurried footfalls splashing through the water sharpened to the slapping of bare feet on stone. William slashed his flashlight around the tunnel, searching.

"Where—" Karl said, but stopped short when his own

light flashed high against the top of the tunnel. Lauren clung to the coved concrete like a spider, her mouth hanging open, tongue lolling, shining red and wet against the light. Then, with a preternatural motion, Lauren leapt from that perch into the darkness.

There came a moaning, a heavy door opened on rusty hinges. A red rectangle of light flashed, then vanished as quickly as it had appeared.

William followed the sound, shooting his light to the center of the tunnel just in time to see a large, iron door set at the center of the raised platform slam shut.

Without a word, Karl and William ran up the concrete slope leading to the door.

"The fuck is going on, Padre?"

"I . . . I don't know. It isn't supposed to work like this. She's supposed to be a channel for spirits, not a fucking vehicle for them." William took hold of the door, but it was heavy and even with all his effort he couldn't open it alone. "Help me, will you?"

Karl cursed under his breath and reached into his pocket.

"You're serious with that coin right now?!"

"Don't fucking rush me, Will. I've got my reasons!" Karl's voice boomed, echoing down off the moldering stone walls. He took a deep breath, flipped the coin and caught it. "Okay, we're good," he said, then reached down and they pulled together.

Karl grunted. "How the fuck did she get this thing open by herself?"

William, straining with all his meager strength, didn't have an answer. The door moaned again, finally swinging wide to allow the two men inside.

It was a long, red hallway. Emergency red bulbs hung from slender cords close to the ceiling. Spray-painted on the walls were words and signs, some that William knew, others he did not. What he knew, even without knowing the full measure of their meaning, was that this place was a housing ground with significant occult power. A place of ritual.

A place consecrated for one, malicious purpose: human sacrifice.

"Unersättlicher hungrig," said William, reading a slash of words illuminated by his flashlight. His ability to translate German was not the best, but he knew those words. And reading them sent a fresh needle of ice into his heart.

"What?" asked Karl.

"Voracious hunger. It's associated with a god of the old world. Moloch."

"Moloch?"

William's vision seemed to lengthen, the fear seizing his mind. "A god who delights in human sacrifice."

"*Fucking* nazis."

From down the rusted, iron walls came a harrowing scream. The scream of the three women.

Then came another voice, a male bellowing in fear.

"Hurry," said William, rushing ahead of Karl.

They ran down the hall, throwing all caution to the wind. Turning a sharp corner they came upon a man sitting with his back against the wall. He clutched at his throat, dark and wet. Blood poured through his fingers down a white, button-down shirt.

William, without thought, bent down to apply pressure to the man's neck.

He was young. Much younger than William. A panicked disbelief in his dying eyes.

"He's done, Will," said Karl. "Come on."

William pressed his hands against the man's neck harder, but the blood kept flowing, running over their fingers. The man took in a deep, gurgling breath.

The young man's irises expanded. His hands relaxed.

Everything was red. The blood, the light. All of it. The

redness reflected in the youth's flat, dead eyes, staring back at William.

More screams erupted from an open doorway ahead of them.

"Will, we have to hurry!"

They bounded down the hall toward the fearful cries. Will and Karl's shoulders clashed together as they tried to barrel through the doorway. It was a strange room, oval in shape. Bodies were littered about the floor, some of them still moving. Others never to move again.

A figure blurred at the edge of William's vision. A sharp pain streaked down his arm. Instinctively, he spun away from the figure, but it kept coming at him. He saw the woman's lunatic smile and the crude, bloody knife she held high above her head.

She screamed, throwing herself at him, ready to bury the knife into his chest.

A thunderous explosion deafened him. The woman's chest blossomed in a red spray, opening her chest and throat, sending her spinning to the ground. William didn't even realize he had fallen over until he felt Karl pulling him to his feet.

Through the ringing in his ears William heard Karl curse.

"Goddamn it!" said Karl, racking a fresh shell into his shotgun.

William blinked away the blood in his eyes. Everything was happening so fast and Lauren, where was Lauren?

He scanned the room. It was filled with rows of folding chairs facing a raised platform. Set upon the platform was a large section of stone, white save for the dark stains that ran down the sides like black ivy. A hand rose from behind the stone, then quickly plunged down. Appeared, then again, shot out of sight.

"Please," a voice pleaded. "Please, don't."

From behind the stone rose the harrowing visage of

Lauren, her face slathered with blood. A smile was on her lips. "Marshal," the three voices said from her lips. "Elder Marshal."

From around the stone crawled a man, his fingers dug into the wood platform, trying to drag himself away from the creature lording over him. He wore a long, white robe, black sigils stitched into the fabric. The man spilled over the lip of the platform onto the hard ground.

Marshal clutched at a massive, writhing wound at his stomach. "Please." Hope filled his features upon seeing Karl and William standing not ten feet away. "Please, help me."

Karl said nothing.

William watched Lauren, who tilted her head to stare at the wounded Elder Marshal.

Eyes bulging like boiled eggs, rheumy with possession, Lauren approached the wounded Molochian priest, admiring the fear in his own eyes.

"Lauren," said William, unsure of what else to say.

The woman ignored him, placing one hand over Marshal's mouth, and with the other, pinched his nose shut. Though he thrashed against her, the powers possessing Lauren were too strong.

"We should—"

Karl cut William off. "We should do nothing. This is what vengeance looks like for the violated, Padre."

William shook his head, and though he wanted to turn away, he found that he could not.

Time lengthened and Marshal's dying took all of it. His muted protest distilled to a low, droning moan. His limbs ceased to thrash, diminishing to little trembling seizures until finally, he stopped moving entirely.

Lauren's possessors released a deep, satisfied exhalation. Through her, they stared into Marshal's blank eyes, shoulders beginning to shake. There came a noise William thought was the sound of the women weeping through Lauren.

167

"It's over," said Karl, turning to William.

The sound coming from Lauren shifted, rising into laughter.

William's brow furrowed, understanding the noise. "Let her go," he commanded.

Lauren snapped her milky-white gaze at him. She shook her head slowly.

"The fuck is going on, Will?" Karl said, and for the first time in his life, William heard an uncertainty in the man's voice.

"The ghosts have what they wanted," replied William. "They're supposed to be laid to rest now. The medium is supposed to come up out of the diviner's well."

"No rest," said the voice of three from Lauren's lips. She closed her eyes and when they opened, the rheumy white was replaced, now all black. "Only suffering, Faust."

A deep chasm opened inside of William's heart. "No," he said.

"Long and hard was the way to get close to you, Hellbane, but we have grown so close. You have something the Master wants. His children," the creature said, joyful malice in her tone.

"Will?" asked Karl.

"She isn't a medium," he replied. "Lauren is possessed. They lied . . . lied to me through Lauren."

"Did you think there would never come an accounting? Did you believe that you could imprison our princes with impunity, Father Faust?"

"Who the fuck is Father Faust?" Karl leveled the shotgun at Lauren.

"It's me," said William. "It's the name they know me by. The name I used to protect myself from . . . "

It all locked into place.

Lauren hadn't suddenly become a medium upon moving to Black Wells. The attack in the nightclub, using William's psychiatrist to find him, manifesting itself to look like a group of vengeful ghosts. All of it had been a lie. A cheat. That's why Sarah's magical room hadn't protected Lauren, it hadn't been an outside oppression trying to get inside her. The demon had been inside her all along, biding its time, gaining his trust. It wasn't the demons inside his mind that attacked him at the Kasdan Archive, that attack had come through Lauren. And the demon had waited inside Lauren until William had given his true name as they had sat at his dinner table together. It learned *how* William was using the power of the sacrament to keep the demons locked up inside his mind. The demon had used Elder Marshal to come into the world, cheating its way through a human sacrifice the Moloch worshiping cult thought was their own god coming into the world, that it might make its way into William's life. And he had fallen for it.

If this was a demon, though, he could open his mind, pull the damnable creature out her before—

And suddenly, before he could open the cage inside his mind, after years of protecting himself from the immortal legions of Hell, a demon spoke William's true name.

"William Carter Daniels."

He shot upright, his muscles tensing so hard he thought his spine might break. William's teeth began to grind together. His eyes squished shut. A tremendous pressure ballooned inside his skull, like his head might suddenly explode.

"Eyes closed, William. No cheating this time," said the demon.

"Let him go, bitch," said Karl. "I'll blow you right back to Hell."

"He doesn't understand, does he, William? Killing this vessel will do nothing. We have all the suffering we need to invade another."

"Don't," William said through clenched teeth. "It will just possess you. Run, Karl. Run!"

"Not a fucking chance, Padre."

"I can feeeeeeeel them," said the demon. "Squirming behind the blood, longing to be free again. You will make them free, exorcist."

The pressure inside William's head swelled, sending him to his knees. "No!" he cried out in pain. He would not relent. Hell could not have back the creature that had taken his wife and child from him. It could not take that from him. He would not allow it.

The demon let out a low hum. "Even with your name, I cannot reach beyond your blood sacrament. The prison within you . . . it stinks of the divine. But it is close to expiring, that too, I can feel. And when it does, the chains will break and again my brothers will be set free. For they are needed, William. The master has such plans for them," said the demon, who then rose and stepped toward him.

"All of this planning, all this waiting, just for this. This little taste of your suffering."

Though he struggled, William felt the barriers inside his mind beginning to crack. He could not hold on much longer. He just needed a moment, if he could open his eyes . . . but the demon's oppression was fully upon him.

"Karl," William managed through the pain. "Rush her!"

The big man didn't hesitate. He dove at Lauren, trying to tackle the woman to the ground.

With impossible speed, she caught the mammoth man as though he weighed nothing, clutching him by the throat.

A hacking sound escaped Karl's mouth, quickly silenced by the creature's crushing grip.

The weight upon William's mind suddenly relaxed. He could open his eyes.

Open the prison doors inside himself.

"Lauren!" William barked.

Their gazes meeting was the creature's first and final mistake since taking up inside Lauren's mind.

William Carter Daniels opened wide his mismatched

eyes, opening the supernatural void that had proved too great for the greatest of Hell's pantheon. And so it would prove too great for this creature.

The trio of demonic voices howled. Slowly. Painfully for both equal oppressors, the demon inside of Lauren Saunders was drawn out like poison from a wound. That poisonous entity screamed, and screamed and screamed. Drawn inside of a red, crystalline jail inside William's mind.

The exorcist felt the demon's terror. The panic and the rage of the thing tried to snake its way around the barriers within his mind. Clenching his fists, his teeth, and squeezing all his willpower into this one effort, this one act, William Carter Daniels, known to the demon world as Father Faust, slammed shut the cell.

He collapsed. The last thing he saw before unconscious took him, was Karl trying to help Lauren to her feet. Panicked and afraid, Lauren looked at her hands. Hands gloved red and wet.

The scream that left her throat was her own.

Chapter Twenty-One

Lauren

"**I**t lied to me," said Lauren. She was sitting in William's office chair, staring out the window onto the cityscape of Black Wells. "Destroyed my life. Made me believe I was a medium. Gave me the ability to travel to that other place. Just to get close to you."

"Yes," said William. "It's my fault. I'm sorry."

Lauren gazed at the Astolat mountains, her eyes tracing the silver ribbon of waters cutting their way through the snow-blanketed Starlight Valley. It was beautiful.

There was a long silence between them.

"What will you do now?" William asked.

The question was incomprehensible. She didn't know what to say. So, she ignored it. "I moved to Black Wells to get away from a bad relationship. To get a fresh start. When I got here, I couldn't believe how beautiful it was. The mountain . . . the river. I thought, this was a place that might have something wonderful waiting for me. But, it didn't. It only had you."

"If I had known," he began. But Lauren had no use for his words.

"It doesn't matter what you would have done, Mr. Daniels. What's done is done."

The exorcist stepped to stand beside her. "I have money. I'll help you move. Go wherever you need to go."

Lauren thought about that for a long time. Where was there to go? Could she just leave this place . . . these experiences behind?

Out there, in the world, there would just be starting over again. Trying to understand another place. She wondered if there were other cities like Black Wells. What if she mistakenly moved to one of them, only to find herself in another, fresh nightmare? The thought chilled her.

"I'm scared to leave," she said. "What will you do now?"

The exorcist shook his head. "There's no end to this for me. Just forward."

Lauren thought about those words for a moment, then said, "I think . . . I think that's how I feel. You saved my life, Mr. Daniels. What happened to me was because of what you're doing here. You won't be able to trust anyone new now."

"I suppose you're right."

Lauren turned away from the mountain and looked up at the exorcist.

He turned to look back at her, his mismatched eyes glassy, brightly shining against the light glancing off the snow outside.

"But, I'm not new anymore. You could trust me."

William shook his head. "Lauren, this life . . . it isn't one I wouldn't advise anyone to have. It's harsh, cruel. Difficult to endure."

"You do. Sarah and Karl, they do."

Through the open office door, Lauren heard the lobby door open and close.

At that sound, William's jaw tensed.

"Mailman," said Lauren.

"Yeah," he replied.

"Part of me hates ever meeting you, Mr. Daniels."

"That's fair."

"But," she said, looking out at the dark Astolats, "the

173

rest of me wants to help you. Help you stop what's happening here."

"I can't . . . " The metal door of the mailbox closing echoed up to the office. Footsteps trailed across the marble floor. The lobby door opened again, then closed.

They were alone again.

"Lauren, I would move heaven and Earth if it meant . . . if it meant changing what's happened. But I can't. And I won't let you—"

"It isn't your choice, William Carter Daniels," said Lauren. "It's mine."

William leaned against his desk, resting his tired frame against it. "It is."

"Downstairs is an envelope. It has your name on it. Whatever is inside, we're going to face it together," she said, placing a gentle hand on his shoulder. "I know you're afraid, but I'm going to ask you to trust me. Trust me with this."

William rested his hand on hers. "More than anyone else," he said. "I do."

Acknowledgments

This book exists in large part due to the love and support of many people. They, each of them, have taught me something about the world and myself in the time spent in their company.

To Becky, Alexander, and Elijah—Thank you for your love. Your patience. And all your many sacrifices that have allowed me to reach this step in this journey. I love each of you.

To Melodie Musgrove—Thank you for your love and friendship and indelible support. You are the very best of what the world has to offer. I love you.

To John McMahon—As always and forever, you remain a sincere, unassailable pillar of both support and physical fitness. There is no one I trust more. I love you.

To Joe Wilkinson—As always and forever, you remain a champion and unflinching supporter of my work, bringing me a happiness I can never fully describe. I love you.

To Sadie Hartmann—What a boon you are, what a surprise. Without your support, this book would not exist as it does. Thank you for believing in me, and yes, all of my love to you as well.

To the wonderful people at Ghoulish Books. Thank you for taking the chance and putting your full support behind this dreamer.

With the most sincere appreciation and the full depth of my heart, you have,

All of my love,

—Carlton Seth Humble, March 1, 2022

About the Author

C.S. Humble is an award-winning American novelist and short story writer. He lives in East Texas. He can be found @cshumble (twitter) or at his website http://cshumble.com.

SPOOKY TALES FROM GHOULISH BOOKS

☐**BELOW | Laurel Hightower**
ISBN: 978-1-943720-69-9 $12.95
A creature feature about a recently divorced woman trying to survive a road trip through the mountains of West Virginia.

☐**MAGGOTS SCREAMING! | Max Booth III**
ISBN: 978-1-943720-68-2 $18.95
On a hot summer weekend in San Antonio, Texas, a father and son bond after discovering three impossible corpses buried in their back yard.

☐**LEECH | John C. Foster**
ISBN: 978-1-943720-70-5 $14.95
Horror / noir mashup about a top secret government agency's most dangerous employee. Doppelgangers, demigods, and revenants, oh my!

☐**ALL THESE SUBTLE DECEITS | C.S. Humble**
ISBN: 978-1-943720-71-2 $14.95
A possessed woman and an exorcist descend into an occult labyrinth of dark forces and oppressive spirits.

☐**RABBITS IN THE GARDEN | Jessica McHugh**
ISBN: 978-1-943720-73-6 $16.95
13-year-old Avery Norton is a crazed killer—according to the staff at Taunton Asylum, anyway. But as she struggles to prove her innocence in the aftermath of gruesome murders spanning the 1950s, Avery discovers there's a darker force keeping her locked away . . . which she calls "Mom."

☐**PERFECT UNION | Cody Goodfellow**
ISBN: 978-1-943720-74-3 $18.95
Three brothers searching the wilderness for their mother instead find a utopian cult that seeks to reinvent society, family . . . humanity

☐**SOFT PLACES | Betty Rocksteady**
ISBN: 978-1-943720-75-0 $14.95
A novella/graphic novel hybrid about a seemingly psychotic
woman who suffers a mysterious head injury.

☐**HARES IN THE HEDGEROW | Jessica McHugh**
ISBN: 978-1-943720-76-7 $21.95
15 years after the events in *Rabbits in the Garden*, Avery
Norton is a ghost. 16-year-old Sophie Dillon doesn't know
anything about the alleged murderer, yet she's haunted
nightly by the same dark urges, which send her on a journey
to uncover her past with the Norton family and to embrace
the future with her spiritual family, the Choir of the Lamb.
But Sophie's devotions can't protect her from the ghosts
waiting in the wings. After all, she's the one they've been
waiting for.

Not all titles available for immediate shipping. All credit card
purchases must be made online at GhoulishBooks.com.
Shipping is 5.80 for one book and an additional dollar for each
additional book. Contact us for international shipping prices.
All checks and money orders should be made payable to
Perpetual Motion Machine Publishing.

Ghoulish Books
PO Box 1104
Cibolo, TX 78108

Ship to:

Name _____

Address_____

City_____ State_____ Zip _____

Phone Number _____

Book Total: $_____

Shipping Total: $_____

Grand Total: $_____

Patreon:
www.patreon.com/pmmpublishing

Website:
www.PerpetualPublishing.com

Facebook:
www.facebook.com/PerpetualPublishing

Twitter:
@PMMPublishing

Newsletter:
www.PMMPNews.com

Email Us:
Contact@PerpetualPublishing.com

PERPETUAL MOTION MACHINE PUBLISHING

Patreon:
www.patreon.com/pmmpublishing

Website:
www.PerpetualPublishing.com

Facebook:
www.facebook.com/PerpetualPublishing

Twitter:
@PMMPublishing

Newsletter:
www.PMMPNews.com

Email Us:
Contact@PerpetualPublishing.com

CPSIA information can be obtained
at www.ICGtesting.com
Printed in the USA
BVHW060626090322
630953BV00006B/19

9 781943 720712